The Dam Committee

arl H. Smith

The Dam Committee

Earl H. Smith

North
Country
Press

Library of Congress Control Number 2011937124

ISBN 978-0-945980-96-4

For John, Alexandria, Emily and Aidan

Acknowledgments

I am especially grateful to Patricia Newell, publisher at North Country Press, who was willing to take a chance on a first-time novelist and whose skill and guidance have been most appreciated. Thanks as well to Anne Nelson, a splendid editor; Gerry Boyle, one of Maine's finest mystery writers and an endless source of advice and encouragement; Bill Wyman, a novelist, good friend and mentor; Oz Ellis, a veteran engineer who shared his understanding of dams and Tainter gates; Michial Heino, retired Maine State Trooper, who knows much of crime and guns; the artist Kathy Speight Kraynak, and many others, including neighbors and other friends who unwittingly contributed to the amalgam of the characters in this book. I must also acknowledge Nicholas, my Golden Retriever, who filled in many of the details of the story; and not least, my wife, Barbara, who endlessly abides the idiosyncrasies of a writer.

1

Harry stood in the narrow hallway, blindly scuffing at his worn Bean boots as he peered at the barometer on the wall. For most of his thirty years he hadn't had a bit of interest in keeping track of the fickle Maine weather, but now, as the new head of the Belfry Dam Committee, he felt an obligation to be out in front of every change. He took careful notes during Jim Pupo's evening weather report on Channel Seven and, because Pupo was often quite unreliable, fine-tuned a forecast for Belfry Village by gauging the movements of local birds and squirrels, the bend of the balsam stick outside the bathroom window, and the feel of his own bones.

The barometer was the newest tool in his prediction repertoire, and tonight he fully expected it would warn him of another winter storm. Belfry had skipped the customary January thaw, and now, the last Friday of March, snowdrifts were mounded high over the backyard fences, giant frozen stalactites clung to the eaves of the house, and out in front, Grand Pond was still locked in two solid feet of steely blue ice.

Diane had been straightening up after supper and heard her husband's weather mumbling all the way from the kitchen. Endlessly tickled by his new preoccupation with precipitation, she came and stood on tiptoes to peek over his shoulder. "See," she said, tapping a wet finger on the glass. "It's rising. Fair weather's coming. Spring is on the way."

Harry frowned, then bent to pat the dog, Winston, who had been nervously dodging Harry's flopping boots while waiting for his evening walk. "Don't be silly," Harry said, looking up. "A few more good storms coming, then a big runoff. After that, mud. Lots of gawddamn mud. Then, maybe, just maybe, we'll get to spring."

Diane's brown eyes flashed. "I swear," she said, "this entire village is in one giant funk. Hummer was miffed when I forgot my mailbox key this morning, and Malvine carried on because my library book was a day late. Worse than that, she was downright snippy when I couldn't tell her the exact minute Doc O'Neil's coming home."

Harry leaned against the doorframe. "You never get it," he said, fumbling with the buttons on his Mackinaw, "moods around these parts are both cyclical and contagious."

At that, Winston let out a long, mournful groan and flopped down onto the floor. Named long before anyone could have possibly known he would grow up statesmanlike and impatient, the Golden Retriever knew very well when Harry was off on another life-meaning screed. Harry ignored him. "After Labor Day," he explained, "folks around here are quite cheerful because the summer people have gone. There's plenty of laughing and backslapping all over town. Most years, these good spirits hold up right through the holidays, even into January." He paused, raised a finger. "But then, around Ground Hog Day, especially when the winter drags, attitudes begin going downhill, real fast."

"Well now, Harry Crockett," Diane grinned, "we can all be most grateful that these terrible mood swings don't affect you." She poked at his chest. "You're fussy year round."

"Can't help it," he said. "But still, you're making too much of this. The postmaster is meant to get upset when folks forget their keys. It's government regulation; else people would stop bringing their keys at all. As for Mal Grandbush, she's never happy, no matter what time of year, until she's sucked the last drop of gossip out of everybody she meets." He thought for a second. "Besides, you couldn't possibly have told her when Doc's coming home. Nobody knows. Last time Nibber and I checked in with Salome, Tuesday I think it was, she told us he'd called from Ray Brook to say he had some business to take care of and might not be home until Saturday. That's tomorrow."

"*Business*?" Diane made a face. "What kind of business could a man have when he's been locked up for three years?"

Harry shrugged. "Anyway, I do know one thing: After tonight, Doc can take care of Salome all by himself. Winston likes dropping in on her all the time, but Nibber and I have had our fill of it."

"Reminds me," Diane said, handing Harry his mittens and adjusting his wool cap squarely over his ears, "see if our handyman friend plans to join us for supper tomorrow at the Sunrise. It's Karaoke Night, don't forget."

"Don't worry," Harry said. "Nibber would never miss his meatloaf, much less a chance to be with Debbie Swift, your dam committee partner and his all-time favorite waitress."

"Well then, tell him to wear something nice," Diane cautioned. "He sometimes shows up in the worst sorts of things, even when he plans to schmooze with Debbie."

"Doesn't have anything nice," Harry shot back as he and Winston headed out the door.

* * * *

The dog led the familiar way down the driveway and onto Shore Drive, a gravel road that meandered the full east side of Herman Point, a long finger of land jutting due north into Grand Pond. A smaller spur served the west shore, but its entrance was up near the highway, a half-mile away. On foot from the Crockett's, it was quicker to leave Shore Road after a short way and take an almost hidden trail that sliced left through the woods and up to Nibber's cabin.

Weighed by a wet afternoon snow, branches of hemlock drooped over the path, and Harry walked with his hands in front, brushing limbs to keep the slush from falling down his neck. Winston loped on ahead, circling back now and then to grumble about the slow pace. On the dog's third return, Harry brushed the snow from a flat place on a crumbling stone wall and sat down to rest.

The wall had once smartly marked the north boundary of the Nabroski property, in the days when Nibber's family farm stretched in a broad swath across the point, from shore to shore. That was twenty years ago. These days, the stone line served only to mark the survey points of several smaller, new parcels of land.

Diane liked to say Nibber's life story read like a Greek tragedy, and while Harry knew very little about the Greeks, it sounded right to him. Nibber's mother died when he was a kid, and soon after, the farm, like many others in the valley, began to fail. To make ends meet, Nibber's father sold the property along the west shore to an eager lawyer from Connecticut and took on every odd job he could find. They might have made it, but the misery didn't end. The old man died of a heart attack the year Nibber and Harry finished high school, and within a month, Nibber's sister up and married a man she barely knew and moved away. Nibber carried on as Belfry's Jack-of-all-trades, but he was always short of money and, to settle up with his sister, sold the land along the entire east shore. Now, all that was left of the once grand farm was a scraggly plot high on the ridge, where Nibber had his tiny cabin.

Playing the story out in his head put Harry into a frump, and his spirits didn't lift until he topped the ridge and spotted his grinning friend, perched astride a snowmobile parked under the sagging roof of the open cabin porch. A single, naked bulb swung in the breeze over his head, casting a pale glow over the cluttered yard where carcasses of two discarded snowmobiles sat buried under humps of snow. Near the cabin, a pole chain-fall teepee straddled an engineless, rusting Chevy pickup, still sitting where it had died.

Nibber saw them coming, put two fingers to his mouth, and sent a shrill whistle into the thin night air. Winston took off like a skunk on fire. With an accelerator far better than his brakes, he reached the porch at full tilt and launched himself into Nibber's lap, sending them both clattering to the floor, scattering empty gas cans and beer bottles as they rolled in joyful reunion.

Harry walked gingerly up the porch steps that Nibber had purposefully packed with snow to fashion a ramp for the dented Yamaha. "Trail's awful," Harry complained. "Like these cussed steps."

Nibber rose up to his full six feet, whopped a solid greeting on Harry's back. "Didn't get out today, and besides, she'll all be gone soon enough," he said, gesturing over the drifts. "Spring is on the way."

For the second time in an hour Harry was called upon to adjust long-range weather predictions, and he was quick. "As dam custodian, you should know better," he scolded. "Your friend Debbie, too, even though she's not yet quite up to speed on the whole dam business."

"We're just fine," Nibber said. "Make a perfect committee. Debbie asks the questions, I answer them, and you fuss about everything else."

"Be serious," Harry said. "It's downright scary to think that the three of us are all that stand between smooth flows and floods around here."

Nibber didn't answer, looked down as he re-arranged his shabby canvas coat and wrestled with the broken zipper. Harry changed the subject. "Diane wants to be sure you're coming to the Sunrise tomorrow night."

"I'll be there," Nibber said, "but a better question is where we'll be going for our nightly walks after Doc gets home." He paused. "Or, who knows? Maybe he won't come home after all." He thought some more. "Come to think of it, might be better for Salome if he didn't."

* * * *

The weather had cleared, and a quarter moon shed light enough for them to see their way around the back of the cabin and start across the ridge. Winston broke trail. Harry broke the silence. "I've never really known quite what to make of Salome," he said. "Much less, Doc. Only met him once, when Diane and I went for a neighborly greeting soon after they moved in. Took an apple pie and bottle of wine, sat on the porch. Doc kept going inside to talk on the phone. Hardly spoke to us. For all I know, you could be right. She probably *would* be better off without him."

"He sure was a mystery man at first," Nibber said, "but that didn't last long." They stopped for a moment to rest, and Harry remembered the summer four years before when the O'Neils bought the Gorman house on the shore. The old couple was beginning to find it hard to care for the place and they were pleased when it sold the very first day the listing appeared in the *Boston Globe*. A lawyer representing the O'Neils called to say his clients would buy the house, sight unseen, and pay the asking price. It was that quick. The Gormans moved out and the O'Neils moved in within a month.

At the time, Harry remembered, the village was abuzz with questions about its newest neighbors. For one thing, nobody had the foggiest idea what Doc did for a living. Hummer, always uneasy when he didn't know most everything about everybody, took a stab at it when he bravely announced to the post office lobby assembly one morning that Doc was into medicine. Given the man's nickname, Nibber had allowed as how it wasn't a very clever guess, but as things turned out, the postmaster was partly right. Doc was in the allied field of pharmaceuticals.

The truth came on a January morning, when a front-page story in the *Watford Journal* reported that Gregory 'Doc' O'Neil, once of Chelsea, Massachusetts, and more recently of Belfry, was arrested by state and federal agents on the Maine Turnpike, near Gray. The story said he had ten kilograms of powder cocaine in his van and several thousand dollars in cash in his pocket.

In Belfry, where crime stories normally had to do with siphoned gas tanks, exceeded game bag limits, and stolen ATVs, Doc's arrest was a sensation. The *Journal* followed the story closely, even sent a reporter to the trial, a brief open and shut affair where, without a whimper, Doc pleaded guilty and was promptly sentenced to three years in the New York medium security federal penitentiary at Ray Brook.

The day Doc went off to jail, Salome called Nibber and asked him to drain the pipes and close up the place. Most folks thought she was gone for good, but in the spring she called Nibber to say she was coming back again.

"Diane got us into this," Harry said, remembering Salome's surprise return. "Felt sorry for her, I guess. Called her a grass widow, all alone down here on the shore with nobody to look after her." It was true. Both by nature and the profit of experience, Belfry people were wary of strangers. To make matters worse, a well-clipped newspaper story, published at the time of the trial, revealed that Salome had been a topless dancer in Chelsea when she first met Doc, and that her career had blossomed after they married and moved to Revere Beach. In the gossipy dither that followed, there were a few in Belfry who found their interest in Salome had piqued, but most used the revelation as another excuse to ignore her. Diane was quick to point out at the time that nothing in the news reports or at the trial itself tied Salome to Doc's drug business, and it wasn't right to expect Salome to fend for herself.

Soon after, Harry and Nibber began their vigil. They stopped by every day or so to make small talk and do an odd job or two, or sometimes they only walked to the top of the ridge and looked down to check for lights in the windows and smoke from the chimney. That's exactly what they planned to do tonight. Doc would be home soon enough, and it was already late.

* * * *

The north-facing slope was packed with snow, and they struggled for a time before reaching the top of the ridge. Warming temperatures had begun to evaporate the snow, and a lacy mist shimmered under the half moon.

Harry spotted the strange extra light first, and it gave him a start. The fog suddenly became streaked with eerie, sweeping waves of red and blue, weak at first, stronger as they went along. Winston must have seen the odd light, too, because he raced back, tail down, muttering under his breath as he took refuge between Harry's legs.

Straddling the dog, Harry plodded awkwardly behind Nibber to the edge of the clearing where they were startled by the sight of a yellow plastic ribbon blocking their way. Nibber pointed toward the O'Neil house. Floodlights bathed the area, and Harry could see that the warning ribbon was strung around the entire clearing. Several vehicles were parked in the double driveway by the house. Farthest away and first in line was a light-colored sedan he didn't recognize. Behind it were two state cruisers, engines running, blue lights flashing. Nearest, up front, was the familiar restored Army Jeep belonging to Fred "the Deacon" Jalbert, and behind it was a white sheriff's car. Tucked close behind the sheriff was the unmistakable shiny black hearse from the Watford Funeral Home.

"Good grief!" Harry spat out. "Salome's dead!" He turned and glared at Nibber. "And on our watch."

Nibber never hung black crêpe with Harry. "Now don't go gettin' yourself all het up," he said calmly. "We'll just have to wait and see."

2

Light came through every window of the house, and shadows of figures flitted about, upstairs and down. There didn't seem to be anybody outdoors, and Harry thought he might step over the barrier for a closer look. It wouldn't take more than ten seconds to sprint to the unlit corner of the garage. Winston would be wary, but he'd come along. Nibber, who never saw a fence he didn't have the urge to jump, already had one leg hoisted over the ribbon, and Harry was set to follow when a familiar bulky figure rolled into the lights of the clearing.

"This is great," Nibber said, jumping back into the shadows. "Our good buddy, Deputy Sheriff Kelly Hallowell, will tell us everything we need to know."

"Not likely," Harry muttered, watching as the sheriff waddled toward them in her puffy, department-issue winter jacket. "She's a clam when she's in uniform."

"Well, I suppose you could say that *is* a uniform," Nibber observed. "Looks kinda like the Michelin Man to me."

Harry didn't crack a smile, continued watching Kelly, who seemed to follow an earlier set of prints that came from the house up to where they were standing. He hadn't noticed the tracks before and pointed them out to Nibber. "Who was that, you think?"

"The guy who strung the ribbon, I guess."

"Nope. The ribbon goes around. These prints come straight up." Harry bent for a closer look just as Kelly yelled in a most officious voice: "Halt! Who goes there?"

"It's me," Nibber shouted back from the dark side. "The Lone Ranger, with Tonto and my dog, Bullet."

She waited until she got up close. "Smart ass," she barked, playing her flashlight across their faces. "Stay behind the ribbon," she ordered, "and you, too, Winston."

Winston, still crouching between Harry's legs, looked up with a frown. "Now, go look at what you've done," Nibber said, cupping a hand over his eyes to block her light. "You've gone and hurt the dog's feelings. There wasn't a need for the separate warning."

Kelly looked puzzled, and Harry ducked close into her face. "What the hell is going on here?"

"Sorry," she said. "Can't tell you. Need to know, you know." Harry had heard the 'need to know' business before. It was her favorite and most annoying reply whenever anybody asked about police business that only the cops had a need to know.

Harry stooped even closer. "Look here," he said, "you know damn well we've been looking after that woman since her husband went to jail." He pointed to the O'Neil place. "If there's anybody with a need to know, it's us."

Kelly was unmoved. "Sorry," she repeated, dousing her flashlight and placing her hands on her round hips, "can't tell you a thing. This here's a crime scene."

Harry knew she was going to be hard to shake. Even though they'd been pals since the days when she worked for the phone company and hung out with the boys at the Sunrise after work, in her new job as deputy sheriff of Cebennek County, old friendships never trumped sworn duty. He couldn't blame her. The career change hadn't been easy. She'd gone on a crash diet and put lifts in her shoes to get into the police academy, and when she graduated and got this job, she was all-cop, especially in uniform.

Harry decided to come at things a different way. First, he took quick stock of what he already knew. There'd been a crime. Kelly said so. And the Watford hearse plainly announced someone was dead. He stepped back, lowered his voice. "I've been wanting to tell you," he said sweetly, "we Belfry folks sure are lucky to have you keeping the peace around here." Nibber turned and gave Harry a puzzled look. "Always at the ready," Harry continued. "Always first on the scene. Such a comfort when the rest of us go to bed at night." Nibber covered his mouth and pretended to gag.

"So," Harry tip-toed, "what time did you get here?"

She paused, tucked in several chins, and took the bait. "No harm tellin' you that," she said. "A matter of public record. Salome's 911 came at 17:10 and a few seconds later a 10-51 came from Central to respond to a shooting … uh, well, a 10-49, on Herman Point. I was over on the East Road, working a poaching stake. Got here at 17:20. Now, that's really all I can tell you. Don't ask me another thing."

She'd said a lot. Salome had made the 911 call, so she wasn't dead. Knight's General Store had a police scanner, and Harry knew some of the code numbers from a list that hung on the wall. A 10-51 was for all available units. He was pretty sure a 10-49 was a homicide.

"Who's dead?" Nibber knew the numbers, too.

"Can't say." She didn't need to, because at that moment the answer came out the back door of the house. Two men in black trench coats were carrying someone, not very big, in a body bag, on a stretcher.

Harry played a hunch. "What time did Doc get home?"

"Can't say."

Be damned. It was Doc in the bag.

"Didn't stay long, did he?" Nibber quipped.

"Nope," Kelly said, "but, like I said, I can't talk about it. It's time you boys moved along."

Harry had one more question. "Who let the Deacon inside the ribbon?"

"He was here when I arrived," Kelly said. "Salome said she'd called him. He seemed to calm her. State boys let him stay. You know, a man of the cloth and all that."

"If he's a man of the cloth, I'm the Man of La Mancha," Nibber said, bouncing on bowed legs like a man on horseback.

Kelly tried not to grin. "Anyway," she said, "The Deacon does have some standing. And, except for you guys, he's the only one who ever paid any attention to the poor woman."

"Pastoral visits, I'm sure," Harry suggested.

"Whatever," Kelly said. "In any case, he was needed. She was some upset at what she'd done."

Bingo! At what *she'd* done? It clicked. Doc came home early and Salome killed him. But why? Harry decided not to push; Kelly probably didn't know any more than what she'd already spilled out.

The men from the funeral home slammed the back door of the hearse and one of them called across the clearing for Kelly to guide them in turning so they wouldn't need to back down the narrow access road in the dark.

"Gotta go," Kelly said. "Too bad I couldn't help you boys, but you know how it is. Need to know, and all that."

"Yeah, well," Nibber replied, "we know enough to know when we don't need to know."

Harry motioned to Nibber, and they were set to leave when the back door of the house opened again. Salome came out first, head bowed, hands cuffed in front. The Deacon towered over her, one arm draped over her shoulders as two uniformed officers led them to the nearest cruiser. Harry recognized one of the troopers, Aidan Brown from the Watford Barracks, the state officer who got called when the local sheriffs got in over their heads. They watched Brown ease Salome into the back seat of the cruiser and exchange words with the Deacon through the open window before it closed again and the car headed slowly down the access road toward Shore Drive. Kelly backed her patrol car to let the Deacon get out with his army Jeep and fall in line behind the cruiser.

The house lights went out and, in short order, the floodlights were taken down and stowed in the trunk of the second cruiser before it trailed the entourage down the road. The only one left behind was Kelly. "She'll guard the scene," Harry said. "Whose car is that?" He gestured toward the only other car, left up front.

"Doc's rental, I'd guess," Nibber said. "Let's go. Can't learn much more here tonight."

Harry turned to look for Winston, who had mustered the courage to stray a bit and was sniffing and digging a short way off the path, at the edge of the clearing. Harry called out, but the dog paid no attention, and Harry moved off toward the sound.

The moon had nearly disappeared, and the darkness made a sharp contrast to the floodlights of moments ago. Harry waited for his eyes to adjust, then spotted Winston, his front paws sending showers of snow and ice into the air. Harry moved closer and saw something shiny in the shallow hole. It looked like the corner of a metal box. Harry called Nibber, and all three began scraping in the hard snow to free the thing. It didn't take long.

Harry struggled to his feet and brushed the last bit of snow off what appeared to be a perfectly ordinary metal suitcase except for the heavy padlock that dangled from a steel hasp fastened over the standard combination lock. Harry sat the heavy case back down in the snow beside Winston, who seemed to be grinning as he wagged his tail. Harry turned to Nibber. "We'll take it home," he said. "No sense to try getting it open here in the dark."

"No need at all," Nibber said with a grin matching Winston's. "We can be pretty sure it's full of money."

3

They stopped often on the way back, to rest and exchange the heavy suitcase. Cooling temperatures had iced the rutty trail, and an overcast sky made it hard to see. For long stretches, they could only follow the sounds of Winston, happily sniffing his way home. "What if there's no money in here, after all?" Harry sat the suitcase in the snow before answering his own question. "A helluva lot of work for nothing, I'd say."

"Of course it's money," Nibber said, reaching to grab the case. "This thing belongs to Doc, and you can bet it's not filled with dirty laundry."

Harry scowled. "If you're right, we're headed for a mess of real trouble."

"How so?"

"Just you wait and see."

As if to prove Harry's point, a sharp cracking sound suddenly came from a shroud of thick alders, a short way off the trail. Winston turned his head toward the noise, froze in place, and made a low, deep-throated warning. At first, they heard only the sound of their own heavy breathing, but in seconds the snapping continued.

"Not deer," Nibber whispered. "They're up in the hardwood." The noise stopped, then continued, quieter this time. Whoever it was had headed the other way, toward Shore Road.

"It's somebody who saw us," Harry said. "They're following us, sure as rain. After the suitcase. I warned you."

Nibber hesitated. For once, he seemed unsure. "Kelly was the only one we saw, and she was long gone before we found it." He brightened. "Tell you what," he said, "my cabin is just up ahead. We can leave it there."

"Not a chance." Harry was quick. "You don't have any locks."

"Locks are over-rated. Somebody wants in, they get in, locks or not," Nibber said. "Besides, I got nothin' worth stealing."

"Your *Playboy* magazines, maybe?" Harry made a small grin. Nibber was proud of his near-complete set.

"Never mind." Nibber gave up, and they trudged on past the cabin. Going downhill was easier, and Harry began to feel a bit more comfortable when the stillness was broken again, this time by the sudden ignition and roar of an engine, not far away. Nibber dropped the case and all three sprinted the short way toward Shore Drive, vaulting the snowplow banking just in time to catch the taillights of a white pickup, throwing snow and ice as it sped off in the direction of the highway.

"Never seen that truck," Nibber said as they walked back for the suitcase. "I know every damn truck in Belfry, and none of 'em is white."

"We'll stash the suitcase," Harry said. "No sense making a ruckus tonight. They might come back. We can open it in the morning."

They hurried the last hundred yards to Shore Drive, and when they got to the house, Harry opened the overhead garage door and felt his way in the dark, plopping the suitcase under his workbench and covering it with a tattered old tarp. "This is definitely not good," he said as they stepped back outside and pulled down the door, locking it behind them.

"It'll have to do for now," Nibber said, heading down the driveway. "See you in the morning," he waved cheerfully. "For the grand opening."

* * * *

Winston followed Harry on a cautious check around the garage before they went to the house where, through the window, Harry could see Diane, reading in a chair by the woodstove. She waited while Harry removed his coat and boots and arranged them neatly in the closet. "You were gone a long time," she said when he finally drew a footstool up beside her chair. "I was nervous when I heard sirens on the highway awhile back."

Harry didn't answer, turned to Winston who was already perched on his haunches next to her with a look on his face that plainly said he knew something she didn't.

"Doc is dead," Harry finally blurted out.

She sat bolt upright; her book crashed to the floor.

"Salome shot him."

"She never!"

"It's true." He nodded, and then went on to tell her the story, from the confusion at the O'Neil place to the prying of details from the tight-lipped Kelly Hallowell, and from the removal of Doc's body in the Watford hearse to the handcuffed exit of poor Salome.

"And, oh yes, the Deacon was there," Harry added. "Official comforter, I guess you could say."

Diane skipped over the Deacon, her face wrinkled in thought. "Why on earth do you suppose she would shoot him?"

"Must be a reason," Harry admitted.

"And a very good reason indeed. A woman doesn't shoot her husband just because he leaves the toilet seat up."

"Else I'd been dead long ago." Harry glanced at Winston, who was eagerly waiting for the last shoe to drop. Harry obliged. "There's more," he said. "On the way home, we found a big suitcase. We're pretty sure it's full of money."

"You lie!" Diane's eyes popped, and Winston squirmed in delight. "Whose money?"

"Doc's, we think. But of course it might not even be money. We'll open it in the morning. Right now, it's safe in the garage." He paused. "I hope it is."

Diane thought for a full minute. "I think you should have left that suitcase where you found it," she said. "If it's Doc's money, you can be sure there'll soon be people out looking for it." Harry nodded his head gravely, decided not to tell her about the mystery man in the woods. She spoke again. "I think you better give it back."

"To who?" he asked.

"To *whom*." Diane fashioned herself a grammar specialist.

Harry thought she was the one asking the question. "Well, we can't very well give it back to Doc, now can we?"

"Well, then, you'll just have to turn it over to the police."

"We'll see." Harry said.

* * * *

They talked on for a long time, and it was after midnight before they got to bed. Harry couldn't sleep. He got up twice to look out the window and check the garage, and at four he gave up and thrashed around for his slippers. Winston cast a disapproving eye from the middle of the bed as Harry tiptoed out of the room and headed downstairs to the kitchen. It was still dark, and he took a cup of coffee and a flashlight outside to walk around the full garage before padding back upstairs to the tiny room across the hall.

The room had once been a nursery. They'd set it up soon after they were married, when Harry's parents gave them the cottage as a wedding gift. The tiny room sat empty for several years until what had begun as a sign of promise turned into a sad symbol of disappointment. No baby came, and one day last spring, when Diane was off shopping, Harry dismantled the crib and moved it overhead in the garage. The pink and blue room became an office.

Now, seated at his makeshift desk, Harry pulled a thick file from a cardboard box on the floor. The penciled tab said **CROOKS WE HAVE KNOWN**, and in it were news clippings having to do with the hapless adventures of a number of Crockett acquaintances: a Watford priest, defrocked soon after a Boy Scout Jamboree; the former Belfry town manager, jailed for borrowing food pantry funds; and sixteen deer poachers, whose names read like a neighborhood directory, nabbed last September by Deputy Kelly and the local game warden, Hannah Dimble.

Harry paused over the poacher clips, remembering Kelly had said she was on a stakeout when she was called to the O'Neil house. He wondered if maybe she was again keeping an eye on Wilbur Findlay, fresh from jail after doing time as ringleader of the busted poachers. Although Kelly hadn't yet learned to keep her mouth shut about police matters, when it came to investigating she was a dog with a bone. Last fall's stakeout was an example. She'd trailed old Wilbur for weeks before she and Hannah finally moved in for the kill.

Nibber had gotten the story from Kelly over a few beers at the Sunrise. She claimed it was Wilbur's fondness for mountain oysters that did him in. On the night of the bust, Wilbur produced a legal doe permit and loudly protested that everything was in order, and when they opened the freezer, the quantity did indeed seem to match. Even so, Kelly insisted on unwrapping the packages and reassembling the animal right there on the linoleum. Shoulders, loins, rumps, legs, shanks, flanks and brisket all perfectly lined up until she reached to the very bottom and snagged the last two wrapped packages.

"They looked a lot like stuffed Jalapenos," Kelly told Nibber, "but Hannah said they were testicles, and she would know." In fact, there was not just one, but two complete sets. Wilbur spent the winter in the Watford County jail. Hannah gave most of the meat to the food pantry, but Kelly pulled out the mountain oysters for Nibber who, so far as Harry knew, had yet to cook them.

Harry walked to the window. All was quiet. The only sound came from Diane and Winston, snoring in chorus across the hall. He went back to the desk and took out the biggest bundle of clippings in the file, all related to the arrest and trial of Doc O'Neil. He leafed through them until he came to the one he was looking for, a long *Globe* feature, written soon after Doc's sentencing.

The writer, crime reporter Sally Collins, had sources on both sides of the law, and her feature story was based on an interview with Parker Meehan, the FBI agent who led the investigation. It began with kudos from Meehan for the work his task force had done, and went on to explain that O'Neil had been a third-generation laborer on Boston's Big Dig project when he became involved with the city's Black Wharf Gang. The gang had once been a loosely organized band of pimps and petty thieves, the story said, but then broadened its reach by paying off the cops to buy traffic rights in Gloucester Harbor in order to get a foothold in the urban drug trade.

The article said the Black Wharf Gang first came to attention of police investigators when Boston's North End saw an alarming rise in homicides, many of them gang related. Meehan told Collins it was then that Doc began his rise from a gang lackey to one of New England's premier purveyors of illegal drugs. Despite Doc's elevated position, the story explained, he was not well known in the outside world. That, Harry remembered thinking, was why Doc's name never rang any bells in Belfry.

There were two bits of Collins' story that Harry half remembered and wanted to confirm. The first said there had been a falling out between O'Neil and his second in command, Michael "the Nurse" Corrado. Meehan called the Nurse "ambitious and ruthless," and said he was "willing to kill at the drop of a hat." The inside scoop, Meehan said, was that Doc had been steadily siphoning off gang money for himself, and when the Nurse caught on, Doc ran "to the back woods of Maine" where he planned to continue his operation.

The second confirmation came at the very end of the story, where Meehan explained that while the bust did much to improve the sanity of Boston's North End, the task force was disappointed not to have caught Doc with his full bundle of pilfered cash.

"We might have gotten as much as a half-million," Meehan told Collins. "Instead, when we stripped the van on I-95, we found only a few thousand." Meehan said the agents believed Doc might cop a plea, and they might still get the money before the trial, but instead, Collins wrote, "Doc kept his mouth shut and quietly went off to Ray Brook."

Satisfied, Harry put the clippings away. The *Globe* story proved his memory was right. Somewhere, somehow, Doc had hidden a lot of money before he went to jail. Enough money, Harry realized, that neither the feds nor the Nurse would forget about it in three years' time.

4

It was barely six o'clock, and Harry watched patiently through the window as the tops of the tall pines along the far shore began to shimmer in the first light. It was time. He crossed the hallway and stuck his head in the bedroom to fetch Winston, who thumped his tail on the bed, opened one eye and then closed it again. Too early – and much too cold. Harry let him stay, went downstairs, pulled on his coat, and headed for the garage. He could have the suitcase open before Nibber even arrived.

After making a small fire in the Franklin, he waited only long enough to warm his hands before he pulled away the worn tarp and hoisted the suitcase onto the workbench. If he could somehow remove the cussed rivets, then maybe the entire hasp would come off without having to deal with the sturdy padlock.

He took a small box from an overhead shelf, fished out a rusted quarter-inch bit, fixed it to his electric drill, and began to whir away. Within seconds, puffs of white smoke drifted up from the red-hot tip. He spat, made it sizzle, and bore down harder. The blackening bit spun merrily on the surface. He stopped and rummaged around for another bit, longer but sharper, and had barely begun to drill again when the bit suddenly broke through the cover and plunged deep inside the case.

When he pulled it out, tiny shreds of green confetti filled the air.

It was money, for sure, but he was no closer to it than he was when he started.

He warmed his hands in his pockets and puzzled. Even with all eight rivets removed, the extra welding around the hasp seemed like a professional job, and it wasn't likely to break easily. In desperation, he grabbed a large ball peen hammer from over the bench and gave the padlock a number of solid whacks. It flopped angrily around the hasp but wouldn't let go. Harry began to breathe hard. He took off his coat, opened the overhead door, and backed the Toyota outside. After checking to make sure no one was coming, he went back inside and plunked the object of his assault on the floor. The front left wheel of his pickup was perched high on the suitcase when Nibber's Chevy rattled into the driveway.

"What in God's name are you doin'?" Nibber yelled as he hopped out of the cab even as the smoking engine loudly backfired through a few extra turns. "Looks like you really *are* making a mountain out of a molehill." Harry backed the truck down off the suitcase, got out and frowned at the dented cover.

"Tryin' to pop it," he said sheepishly.

"You're making far too much of this," Nibber said as he sorted through a tangle of tools in the bed of the Chevy and fishing out a three-foot bolt cutter. Harry closed the overhead door and hoisted the case back onto the workbench. Nibber quickly applied the cutters, and with a single grunt, the carbon blades sliced through the padlock bar.

"Like soap," he grinned. "Now all we have to do is figure out the combination lock. Can't be hard. They're cheap." Just then, Diane, a heavy coat over her nightgown, came through the side door with Winston, who went quickly to the stove and sat to scratch his ears with his hind paws, shaking the cobwebs.

"Have I missed the opening?" Diane asked, clutching the neck of her coat.

"Nope. Just in time," Nibber said, bending to place an ear close to the lock.

"Looks like Ray Milland in *Safecracker*," Diane said.

"More like Don Knotts in *Shakiest Gun in the West*," Harry said.

Nibber ignored them both, and after the fourth twirl of the first dial, looked up. "Six," he said.

"You sure?" Harry was doubtful.

Nibber nodded and went back to work. Harry, Diane and Winston lined up behind him like crows on a fence, and nobody said a word until Nibber finally stood up straight. "Two more sixes," he announced proudly.

"Wow!" Diane's eyes popped. "Three sixes. Mark of the anti-Christ."

"The what?" Nibber wrinkled his nose.

"Told you," Harry said. "We're in deep trouble."

With all three wheels set to sixes, the lock let go, and the damaged lid made a loud squeak when Nibber pried it open. The air soon filled with the stale smell of old money. Everybody, including Winston, gaped at the stacks of bills, piled front to back, all in tidy, wrapped bundles.

Diane hesitated a moment, then reached in gingerly, pulled out a single stack, and began to riffle through. They watched her lips count to two hundred before she took a measuring tape off the bench and began to calculate. When she finished the first pile, she took another, counted it and measured some more. "There," she said, looking up after a long minute. "Three wide, nine deep. Twenty-seven thousand bills in all." Diane was good at math. "Most are tens and twenties," she said, "but I saw a few fifties." She stopped, did more figuring in her head. "There's at least a half-million in here, no doubt."

* * * *

They stood quietly for a long while, gaping in awe at the pale green stacks. Harry spoke first. "Now what are we going to do?"

"What do you mean?" Nibber grinned from ear to ear. "We're rich!"

"Never mind that right now," Diane said. "First, we have to figure out where we'll keep it while we figure out what to do with it." She gave Harry a stern look. "I'll tell you one thing, mister. It's not coming in *my* house."

"Won't make any difference," Harry said, remembering the mystery man. "Someone's likely to come and tear the place apart to find it, no matter where we put it."

Nibber wasn't listening. Instead, he was surveying the garage. "Up there," he finally said, pointing to the overhead trusses where Harry had long ago fastened a sheet of plywood to make slots for off-season equipment. Right now, the spaces were jammed with fish rods, oars, paddles, and life jackets. Diane said it was still too close for comfort, but admitted she didn't have a better idea. Harry wasn't sure at all, but said nothing as Nibber got the stepladder, climbed up and began shoving things around to make new space. When he was done, the suitcase slid in with barely an inch to spare. "There you go," he said, cramming an old orange life preserver in front for disguise. "Perfect."

"Not so perfect," Harry said, "but it'll have to do for now."

"Another thing," Nibber said as he climbed down the ladder, a serious look on his face. "I was wondering. Do you guys suppose it would be okay to bring Debbie in on this deal?"

Harry frowned. Diane smiled. "I don't see why not," she said. "The girl has a good head. She'd balance things out."

Harry missed the dig and concentrated on the idea. One thing was certain: If they wanted to live through this, they were going to have to keep their mouths shut. Adding another person to the group would multiply the chances of a leak, especially if that person happened to be a waitress at the most popular hangout in town. On the other hand, he remembered Nibber was such a blabbermouth that Debbie was bound to find out anyway.

Diane had warmed to the idea. "I say we include her. If Nibber had any sense," she said, referencing Nibber's poor courtship abilities, "the dear girl would already be a part of our little family."

Harry didn't argue, made it unanimous. "Okay, fine," he said. "We'll tell her tonight at the Sunrise, after the Dam Committee meeting." He looked at his watch. It was eight o'clock. The post office would be open and the newspapers in at Knight's Store. "Let's go catch the local buzz on the murder of poor old Gregory O'Neil," he said.

5

Winston won the race to claim shotgun in Nibber's Chevy, and Harry climbed in the middle, straddling the shifting lever and yelling for Nibber to slow down as they bounced over frost heaves and potholes along Shore Drive. When they reached the intersection and turned onto the paved highway, Harry squirmed sideways to let Nibber shift, and they had begun to pick up speed when Nibber suddenly trounced on the brakes, sending the pickup on a wild slide through the slush before it finally stopped, inches from a leaning mailbox.

"God almighty," Harry yipped, bracing one hand on the windshield and reaching with the other to keep Winston from wedging his head in the open window.

"Look at that!" Nibber pointed toward Lake Lodge, an ambitiously named set of run-down overnight cabins on the right. "Kerri's got customers."

Harry leaned over the dog's shoulder to look. The spinster Kerri Woods made a living entertaining a faithful clientele of sportsmen and taking in occasional tourists who had miscalculated travel distances. Her winter business was slow, but this morning there were two vehicles in the gravel lot. One was a blue sedan with Vermont plates. The other was the white pickup they'd spotted on Shore Drive last night, from Massachusetts.

"Our mystery man," Harry said, "And somebody else that's new. You can bet it's a rented car," he said, nodding at the sedan. "Vermont has more rental cars than cows."

"Friggin' flatlanders, both of 'em." Nibber called all out-of-staters flatlanders, whether the land they came from was flat or not.

"Well now," Harry brightened, "we'll find out who was snooping in the woods last night, after all. Kerri's sure to be in church tomorrow. We'll ask her."

"Church?" Nibber frowned as he spun the tires back onto the blacktop. "I wasn't planning …"

"By the way," Harry interrupted, "don't tell a soul we were on the ridge last night. That would surely make us suspects."

"Suspects of what? We already know who killed Doc."

"Of grand theft," Harry said.

The grave thought served to dampen the conversation until Nibber wheeled the truck into the only open parking space in front of the post office. "Kelly Hallowell saw us," he said. "What if she blabs?"

"I'll take care of that," Harry said half-confidently, reaching for the post office door just as it opened by itself and out came several grim-faced patrons, heads down, grumbling, elbowing one another in a frantic rush to escape. The reason for the mass exodus was just inside the door. Fred "the Deacon" Jalbert was holding forth in the small empty lobby, talking loudly over the boxes to

Hummer Humbolt, trapped on the other side, sorting mail.

"Mornin'," the Deacon said brightly. "God save you."

"God save you, too," Nibber muttered as he edged around the lanky Deacon and bore down on the lobby wastebasket, dumping its contents on the floor.

"Save *me!*" Hummer's mournful voice came from the other side. Harry understood the plea. Hummer and the Deacon were good friends, church brothers and political partners on the far right, but even the patient postmaster sometimes grew weary of the Deacon's blather.

"Can't save you just now," Harry said, fumbling with his mailbox key. "We're in a rush."

Nibber glanced up from the trash. "Anything for me?" he asked Harry. Nibber shared the Crockett mailbox. It saved money, and while the U.S. Postal Service wouldn't have approved, Hummer let it go because Nibber just about lived at the Crocketts', anyway.

"Some junk and a package," Harry said. "What's the package? You send for something?"

"A surprise." Nibber snatched the brown parcel away from Harry. "Tell you later. Save the junk."

The Deacon sidled up to Harry. "Boy, am I tired," he sighed, his eyes begging a follow-up. "And my back aches."

"Why?" Harry took the bait.

"Up all night."

"Why?"

"You didn't hear?" The Deacon was pleased to inform. "Doc O'Neil got shot last night."

"Oh my," Harry feigned surprise. "Is he dead?"

"Well of course he's dead," the Deacon snapped. "If you got a slug from a .357 between the eyes, you'd be dead, too."

Goodness, Harry thought. *A 357! Between the eyes!* He pushed on. "And why are you so tired?"

The Deacon rose up to his full six-feet-four. "I was on a mission for the Lord."

"No kidding," Harry didn't let up.

"It's a long story, and some of it's privileged information, you understand, but Salome was the one who shot Doc. That much is public. It's in the papers this morning. Self-defense it was. She called me right after she'd done it, and I about broke my neck getting over to her place."

The Deacon lived at the far end of the East Road, several miles out of town. "Good thing you have a Jeep," Harry said. "The roads were bad."

"Yes, it's a blessing to have a Jeep. And I'm glad I went, because I was able to help."

"How?"

"Well, we prayed, and stuff like that."

"Stuff like what?" Nibber jumped in.

The Deacon sniffed, didn't answer.

"Amen!" Hummer piped up from the other side before cranking up the volume on the radio and filling the lobby with the ranting of Rush Limbaugh. Harry plugged his ears. Far right radio was standard fare at the post office, and although some had complained about having one-sided politics on government property, Hummer paid no more attention to them than he did to the pleas to update the lobby photograph of Ronald Reagan, on the wall since 1981.

Nibber and Harry slipped out the door, leaving the Deacon alone with Hummer and Limbaugh. "What'd you get?" Harry asked, nodding at the collection of clippings Nibber held in his hand.

"Coupons for beans, tomato sauce, sardines, and Fig Newtons."

Harry shook his head. Nibber was always broke. The problem was that he rarely charged the locals for the small jobs he did in the winter. They couldn't pay anyway, he explained, so he saved the cost of sending bills. In the main, his income came from the well-heeled flatlanders, who, at Nibber's insistence, paid in cash. Even so, Nibber's tax-free dollars always began to run out by spring, and lately, Harry noticed, his friend was coasting his Chevy down the long hills, rationing his beer at the Sunrise, and taking many extra meals at the Crocketts'.

"Here's a few more coupons," Harry said. "Diane will fill in the rest."

* * * *

Across the street, John Knight was shoveling slush away from the lone gas pump in front of his store. He had set up a line of sawhorses along the road, and the unusually large Saturday crowd was parked on both sides, nearly up to the dam.

"We need a traffic cop," John announced. "And a safety officer, too," he said, pointing to a weathered, hand-lettered sign nailed to the street side of the building: **WATCH FOR FALLING ICE**.

Harry, like most everyone else, had forgotten about the sign. John left it up year-round to amuse the tourists, and in the clutter of notices of bean suppers, church raffles and lost dogs, it had long ago lost its shock value. Worse, as John had explained to Harry only yesterday, the notice had become an outright menace to the handful of regulars who took the text literally and had begun to stand under the eaves on warm days, sipping coffee and cheering as great slabs of ice crept over the edge.

Inside, it was easy to see that the overnight murder of Doc O'Neil had done a great deal to lift the locals out of the late winter doldrums. Chattering customers filled the tiny space in front of the counter, and John's wife Allie did her best to keep order while ringing up sales of coffee and doughnuts. Knight kids were everywhere. Harry had never counted them. Four or five ran around and into customers gathered in bunches along the two narrow aisles. In the back, the good old boys huddled around a wooden picnic table they used whenever it was too cold to sit outside.

Nibber whispered that he would cruise the store and do some eavesdropping, and Harry moved to the back where more regulars were gathered around a single copy of the *Watford Journal*, spread out on the table. Harry leaned over to look at the blazing headline:

BOSTON MOBSTER
SLAIN IN BELFRY

He moved closer to read the short story: "Salome O'Neil of Belfry is being held without bail on a charge of murdering her husband, Gregory 'Doc' O'Neil, a former Massachusetts gang leader recently released from New York's Ray Brook prison after serving a three-year sentence for drug dealing and racketeering."

The story went on to say Salome was represented by Tony Pasquale, "a well-known Watford trial lawyer," quoted as saying his client had shot her husband in self-defense, and was "completely innocent" of all charges. Pasquale said she would enter a plea of not guilty at her arraignment, set for Monday in Watford District Court. That was it. Not a word about any missing money. Harry was relieved.

Nibber finished his tour and re-joined Harry by the table. "I have to work on Monday," Harry said. "Maybe you could go for the arraignment?"

"Oh, sure," Nibber nodded as the two moved off to a corner by themselves. "Turns out my Monday schedule is quite flexible."

"What'd you learn?" Harry whispered.

Nibber mumbled into his coffee. "Nothing new. No money talk, but plenty of theories on why she shot him. Over in canned goods, Mal the librarian said she'd heard

Salome had taken up with the Black Wharf Gang, and they hired her to kill him when he got out."

"Mal's a gossip," Harry said. "And a rattlesnake."

Nibber nodded. "In meats, somebody said Doc stewed for three years because she hadn't come to visit, and she'd taken up with somebody else. They claim Salome shot him before he could shoot her."

"Possible, but not likely," Harry said.

"And then, there's poor Henry McLaughlin," Nibber went on. "He was over by the booze rack, fondling a bottle of Jack and telling everybody not to worry, that he'd get the whole story from his trooper friend, Aidan Brown."

"Yikes!" Harry sent a slop of coffee down the front of his jacket. "If Aidan finds out from Kelly that we were on the ridge last night, he's likely to spill the beans to Henry, and Henry talks like a parrot ... even when he's sober."

Nibber shrugged. "Nothin' more to learn here. Let's go."

They turned to leave just as a shout came from the back of the store. "Hey boys, hold on!" It was Jeff Molony. Harry gave Nibber a fearful glance, wary of his reaction. Molony was a newcomer to Belfry, in town barely ten years. Nibber didn't like him at all, and with good reason. The man had come to town with a wad of money and had quickly built a brisk business of buying lake properties and farms from hard-up locals, cutting them into small pieces, and selling lots to wealthy flatlanders. Nibber had no use for land developers in any case, and Molony ranked lowest of the low. He'd arrived on the scene just when Nibber decided to sell the east shore property, and convinced Nibber to sell the land to him, to get the money right away, and save the cost of a broker. Six months later, Molony re-sold the property for twice what he paid. After that, Nibber gave the man a nickname, and wasn't bashful about using it to his face.

"Cripes. What da ya suppose Bolony wants now?" Nibber grumbled as the short man's bald head disappeared in a clot of customers near the meat counter.

"Dunno," Harry said, following Molony's wake until he reappeared again, much closer. "Something to do with the dam, no doubt." Molony had a family compound on Finger Lake, along the outflow of the dam, and he crabbed endlessly about the water level. It was too high or too low, or the Dam Committee had waited too long or not long enough to make adjustments. The complaints were one thing, but Molony lodged them in public, from one end of town to the other.

Although the dam gate hadn't been moved since the fall drawdown, Harry figured Molony had found some dam thing to fuss about, and he feared the meeting wouldn't be pretty. Nibber was sensitive about dam complaints, and most every discussion with Molony ended up in a shouting match. On top of that, Nibber was at the moment especially aggravated because Molony had begun to hang around the Sunrise, trying to sweet-talk Debbie into selling him the family farm. The very idea drove both Nibber and Harry nuts, especially because Debbie desperately needed money and, they knew, was finding Molony's offer more tempting all the time.

Harry looked toward the door, but milling customers blocked the way. It was too late, anyway. Bolony was on top of them. "How you boys doin'?" His voice was syrupy.

"What do you want?" Nibber skipped the niceties.

Molony kept his smile. "I know you two boys are close to Salome O'Neil," he slurped, "and it looks to me like she might be wanting to sell her place over near you." He paused. "I was hoping you guys might put in a good word for me."

Harry watched the hair stand up on Nibber's scrawny neck. "Listen here, Bolony." Nibber spat the words from a dangerously close distance. "Suppose you tell me why you think the poor woman would want to stand trial for murdering her husband and get screwed by the likes of you all at the same time?"

The words hung in the air. The buzzing store grew quiet. Harry cringed. Molony bristled. "You're meshuga," he finally muttered, turning on his heels and pushing through customers toward the door.

Nibber looked puzzled, then shrugged. "You, too!" he yelled, nodding in satisfaction.

6

Harry brought a half plain sugared doughnut back to the truck, and Winston jumped out to eat while Harry clambered in over the shift lever. Nibber was still fuming over the encounter at Knight's, and when they were all settled and headed home, he growled over the steering wheel. "The man's idiotic." He looked at Harry. "And what's meshuga, anyway?"

"Idiotic, I think." Harry was quite certain.

"Easy for him to say." Nibber bobbed his head. "I can't stand him and his big words," he said, "and I can't stand that preachy sidekick of his, either." Winston nodded in agreement as he wiped crumbs out of his teeth with his long tongue.

Harry, for once, took the positive view. "Well, at least the Deacon's harmless."

Nibber wouldn't let go. "A man who thinks he knows more than everybody else is not harmless. He's downright dangerous."

"I think you're just a little edgy because of the money," Harry said, patting Nibber's knee. "You'll feel a whole lot better after we sort things out tonight at the Sunrise." He hadn't convinced himself, and nobody spoke until they neared Lake Lodge. This time it was Harry who pointed into the parking lot. Both the white pickup and the rental car were gone.

"Can't be far," Harry said. "Either of 'em."

"Exactly who are these people, anyway?" Nibber asked.

"I'd say one's a cop and the other's a crook." Harry was surprised by his own quick answer. "Most likely, they don't even know each other. Just both happen to check in at Kerri's." He paused to admire his developing theory. "No matter who they are, you can be damn sure they're both out looking for the damn suitcase."

"We'll be just fine if we don't make any mistakes," Nibber said as they turned onto Shore Drive where the warming sun had made a muddy soup, held in the middle of the road by the frozen bankings.

"My point exactly," Harry said, clutching the seat as Nibber wrenched from side to side, dodging the deepest ruts. "As you well know, we rarely avoid mistakes."

The accumulated snow made the road narrower than usual, and in most places it was not possible for two cars to pass. As they neared the fork leading up the ridge, Harry bolted straight up and shouted a warning. The white pickup was pulled tight to the side of the road in a short space where the plow had widened the corner.

"He's back!" Harry winced as Nibber inched past the parked truck and headed up the forked road toward the cabin.

"The man's up here somewhere, for sure." Nibber said. "What say we take a walk and see if we can find him?"

Harry wasn't at all sure. "For the love of Pete, wouldn't that be just the kind of mistake we're trying to avoid?"

"Nah." Nibber grinned. "So far's I know, there's no law that says a body can't take a walk in the woods."

When they pulled into the poorly defined driveway, Winston jumped out, ran to the back of the truck and began making circles. "Don't look," Harry warned. "It embarrasses him."

They waited, backs turned, and then headed up the ridge. Water was running over the melting ice, and the path was slippery. As they gingerly picked their way, Harry raised the subject of the *Globe* article he'd resurrected in the middle of the night. "Remember that interview the Boston reporter Collins had with the FBI guy Meehan?"

Nibber nodded. Harry continued. "I dug it up last night, and a few things set me thinking about this mess we're in. For one thing, the G-man was quoted as saying he'd hoped to catch Doc with a pile of money. You can be sure that's the money we've got in the rafters. For another, the agent had a whole lot to say about the Black Wharf Gang and the man called the Nurse. Real name's Michael Corrado. He's one nasty bastard who got crossways with Doc. Now, what would you suppose has become of him?"

Nibber didn't answer, and the two picked their way along, stopping now and then to check for fresh footprints. There weren't any. "And then there's

Salome," Harry went on. "She hasn't forgotten about that money, you can bet."

"Maybe that's why she shot him," Nibber offered.

"Maybe," Harry said, "but it didn't do her a helluva lot of good if she did."

The conversation was interrupted when Winston let out a happy yelp and, tail wagging, raced down the wooded slope toward the clearing. Harry called him back, but it was no use, and the two followed until Nibber suddenly spread his arms wide, blocking the path. "Sweet Jesus," he turned and whispered, "it's him!"

Harry pulled down Nibber's arm for a look. A man in a tan overcoat was standing at the edge of the clearing, back toward them, scuffing in the snow at the exact spot where they had dug out the suitcase the night before.

"Let's get outta here!" Harry hissed.

"Too late," Nibber said. "He's seen us." The man had turned and was watching Winston come toward him at a full gallop. "Keep walking. Act natural. Anyway, we can't leave Winston."

"This is most definitely one of those mistakes we were trying to avoid," Harry muttered as they shuffled on, more slowly than before, watching the man casually smooth the snow with his boots as Winston bore down. Harry half expected a crash, but at the last instant the dog slowed and crept in cautiously, low to the ground, until the man finally put out his hand and bent down, sending Winston into a dancing frenzy.

Harry looked beyond, into the clearing. The yellow police ribbons were still up, but he didn't see any cars.

Even Kelly's cruiser and Doc's rental were gone. The man must have parked his truck at the fork and come up by the way of the O'Neil driveway, crossing the open land in the same footsteps Kelly followed last night.

The man kept his head bowed as they neared, focusing his attention on Winston, who was by this time on his back in the wet snow, legs in the air. "Nice dog," he said, scratching Winston's belly without looking up. "And well fed, too."

Winston's legs froze in midair, and he raised his head with a kind of sneer. Harry broke the awkward moment. "Mornin'." His voice cracked, and he hoped the man didn't notice. "I'm Harry, and this is my friend Nibber. And this here's Winston," he said, pointing to the dog. "He's naturally big-boned." Winston, satisfied with the vindication, resumed wiggling.

Harry stuck out his hand in greeting. The man grabbed it and hung on tight, fixing a cold stare at Harry, who felt a chill when he saw a long, red scar that ran across the man's left cheek.

"You boys from around here?" The man didn't give his name.

"Yup." Nibber answered.

"Come up here often?"

Nibber yupped again.

"Up here last night?"

Harry was set to tell the truth when Nibber lied. "Nope."

The information seemed to be going all in the same direction, and Harry tried to swap things around. "Where you from, and why are you here?" he blurted.

The man grinned, sending the ugly scar in an upward arc. "I'm from Watford," he said. "Read about the murder in the paper this morning. Thought I might drive over for a look."

Lying bastard, Harry thought. *We've seen his white truck three times since last night. Besides, Watford folks don't wear Massachusetts plates.*

Harry was about to pose a follow-up when the man put an end to it. "Nice meeting you," he clipped as he turned to walk back across the clearing.

"Same here," Harry spoke into thin air as Winston flipped right side up, considered his options, then decided to rejoin Harry and Nibber for the walk back up the ridge.

"You know what I think?" Harry said quietly as he watched the man disappear around the corner of the house.

"Yup."

"You do?"

"Yup." Nibber turned with a wry grin. "We just met the Nurse."

7

The Sunrise was always packed on Karaoke Night, and when Harry and Diane arrived soon after six, the parking lot was already filled up with beaters and gun-racked pickups. Harry pulled the Toyota tight to the banking across the road, and when they got out, he pointed to the neon rooftop sign. The last red letter of '*Sunrise Grillé*' was still out.

"It died soon after Emily bought the place," Diane said. "And you've nagged her about it the full two years." She raised her hand. "Give it up. You know she's never going to get it fixed."

Harry knew she was right. Emily used to say it would cost too much to send someone up onto the roof, but the real truth was that she knew the place was never going to measure up as a French restaurant. She had once dreamed of running a high-end place for summer tourists, and her first menu included things like coq au vin, potage du soir, and steak au poivre, but it never worked. Only a handful of flatlanders ever came in, and the locals weren't about to eat anything they couldn't pronounce. These days, the French offerings were limited to egg toast for breakfast and deep fried potato strips all day long.

The French dream, Harry knew, was further doomed when, soon after Emily opened, Chuck Greaver bought the Belfry Inn on nearby Mosher Stream. Chuck had never meant to compete, but one night, after an especially poor meal, he stormed into the Inn's kitchen to confront the owner and came out with the deed. The restaurant became an instant summer success. Folks said Chuck was twice blessed: he had the gift of gab, and his wife Suzette was a fine French cook. Tourists were flattered by his charm, agreed with his most conservative political views, and didn't mind paying extra for *haut cuisine*.

Meanwhile, Emily did a steady business catering to the townies, selling dawn breakfasts to the sports, lunch specials to the working crowd, and plenty of beer when Boston teams were on the flat screen above the bar.

Inside, it was quickly evident that Emily was already set up for the coming St. Patrick's Day celebration when she would put green dye in the beer and the local rednecks would play Irish for a day. Shamrocks were duct-taped to the long mirror behind the bar, and a stuffed green leprechaun danced from the wagon wheel chandelier in the center of the big, open room. The bar stools were filled with the usual suspects, and several tables were pushed together under the leprechaun where the Gammon family huddled around Harry's boss, Gus, seated at the head of the arrangement, wearing a pointy paper hat.

Gus Gammon was special to Harry. The old man had not only taken him under his wing at the sawmill, but he'd also given Harry a strong appreciation of Belfry's past, when city folks came by the trainload to fish the lakes, filling the boarding houses up and down Main Street. "Happy birthday," Harry said as he bent to give Gus a hug.

"Eighty today," Gus said, pointing to the black balloons floating above his chair. "Can't believe it." Diane pecked him on the cheek before she and Harry made their way toward the back corner, where Nibber held their customary booth.

"You've got a nib on your shirt, already," Diane said, pointing to Nibber's belly. Nibber often wore roadmaps of recent meals on his shirts, and his pattern was so regular that Sunrise patrons long ago named all such food splotches, on anybody, in his honor. Tonight's first nib was a quarter-sized blotch of catsup he had obviously tried to wipe off with a napkin, leaving a long, red Nike-like swash. Above the nib, Harry noticed an undecipherable logo Nibber now attempted to hide with one hand while reaching under the table with the other.

"Here," Nibber said, plopping the half-opened package in front of Harry. "It's the surprise that came in the morning mail. This one's for you. Same as mine," he said proudly, "except yours is clean."

"Gee, thanks." Harry held up the white shirt with bold black letters on the front: **BELFRY DAM COMMITTEE.**

"We needed uniforms," Nibber explained. "To get respect." He winked as he jammed the remaining T-shirt back in the package. "Got Debbie one, too. A small. Can't wait 'til she tries it."

"Shame on you," Diane shook her finger. "She's at least a medium." She was set to go on when she was drowned out by the screech of an amplifier in the front of the room where Durwood Green, decked out in a shabby, worn tux, pawed through a tattered cardboard box of CDs, setting up for karaoke.

The squawking was a cue, and Emily instantly came out of the kitchen, dimmed the chandelier, and flicked the switch for the lone floodlight overhead. The sudden heat dissolved a week's collection of cobwebs and sent a thin puff of white smoke wafting to the ceiling.

As if by magic, the bright light suddenly revealed the shapely form of Darlene Ruff, perched smartly on the singing stool. A few years before, as a barfly at the Chez Marseille in Watford, Darlene had easily come to know all of the boys in the band, and one night, the story went, they invited her to sit in. The Marseille faithful loved it, and it wasn't long before she had built a surprising reputation for herself, and for her singing.

Emily first learned about Darlene from the bar regulars at the Sunrise, and was delighted when, in return for a free meal and an open bar tab, Darlene agreed to serve as bait on Karaoke Night. She was perfect. She required no liquid courage to get up and sing, and her lead-off position assured big bar tabs and a long line of eager participants.

Tonight, Darlene wore ruby red lipstick and plenty of rouge, and her well-varnished, once-blond hair was piled high on her head. Her most prominent features seemed to defy gravity as they smiled warmly over the top of a gaping, lacy, white blouse.

Durwood punched in the first CD, and Darlene tugged up her short, tight, black skirt and began to sing. The good old boys at the bar turned in unison, gazing in slack-jawed admiration as they fondled frothy beer mugs in their laps. "Ain't she sumthin'?" Nibber whispered.

"*Isn't* she?" Diane frowned.

"Yes, indeed," Nibber replied as Darlene crooned a breathy Patsy Cline rendition of *Crazy*. "Could have been a professional."

"Already is," Harry observed. "Gets paid, doesn't she?"

"If free meatloaf and a pint of Jack make you a pro." The cheerful voice came from behind, where Debbie was taking orders in the next booth. Long legs in tight jeans, she came around and playfully slid in next to Nibber.

"Can't stop but a minute," she said, smiling sweetly and flipping her black ponytail. "I'm out straight."

Nibber withered in admiration. "Me, too," he sighed.

"Oh, for God's sake," Diane groaned, shaking her head. "We'll have the usual. Caesar with chicken for me. Rare burger for Harry."

"With a pat of butter, onion rings, and beer." Debbie wrote it all down.

"Wait!" Nibber reached under the table and fished out the last uniform. "This is for you."

"Oh, Nibberrrr." Debbie purred, holding it up. "You're sooo sweet. I'll put it on when I get a break."

"Can't wait," Nibber beamed.

Debbie moved on just as Kelly Hallowell waddled through the front door, looking disheveled and exhausted. Up all night, Harry figured, guarding the crime scene.

The deputy squeezed sideways between tables, and as she edged past the booth, her holster splayed horizontally from her hip. The business end of her sidearm pointed directly at Nibber's head, and he jumped to his feet in mock horror. "Don't shoot," he yelled, both hands over his head. "I surrender." Heads turned. Kelly bent down and glared into Nibber's face.

"Maybe I will," she hissed, "or, better yet, maybe I'll ring you up on a Section 4572."

"A what?" Nibber laughed, sat down and dabbed at another nib on his new shirt.

"Sexual harassment," Kelly said, winking at Diane, who nodded agreement.

"Just kidding," Nibber said, still laughing. Kelly wagged her longest finger behind her back as she waddled off to the last empty table, where she draped her uniform jacket on the back of a chair and shuffled off toward the unisex bathroom at the end of the bar.

"Good job, you idiot." Harry shook his head at Nibber. "Just when I needed to ask her a favor."

"Oh, yeah." Nibber made a face. "Forgot."

Harry slid out and tracked Kelly, catching her just outside the occupied bathroom where, on the wall by the door, was a cheaply framed snapshot of Nibber with a scrawled label that said *First Prize, Halloween Costume Party*. The photo commemorated Nibber's accidental participation in last fall's Sunrise Halloween party for the kids. He'd stopped by just as the kids were set to vote for the best costume, and his grizzly three-day beard, tattered baseball cap on backwards, and colorful nibs on his favorite Red Sox shirt, made him appear to be a bona fide contestant. The kids promptly voted him first prize. Debbie took the picture, and Emily hung it on the wall where it had delighted restroom patrons all winter long.

"He means well," Harry said, pointing to the picture. Kelly scowled, then smiled, and was about to offer her opinion when Mal Grandbush came out the bathroom door.

"Well now, lookie who's here," the librarian said, eyes flashing in delight, "the absolute perfect person to fill us in on whatever happened over on Herman Point last night."

"I'm not the perfect person," Kelly scowled. "You'll have to ask …" She stopped, looked at Harry, then went on. "You'll have to wait until you read about it in the paper." Harry exhaled.

Mal adjusted her long skirt and leaned into Kelly's face to whisper. "I hear dear Salome got herself pregnant while her husband was in jail. She shot him before he could find out."

"Good lord!" Harry grunted. "That's crazy." Mal glared at him, sniffed, and walked off. Harry motioned Kelly toward the door. "You're next," he said, "but first, that old biddy reminds me of something." He tried to be casual.

"Of what?"

"Of seeing you on the ridge last night," Harry said. "I'd be ever so grateful if you didn't tell anybody we were up that way. You know how people are around here. We'd be pestered to death with questions we wouldn't know how to answer."

"Not to worry," Kelly said. "You know me. That kind of stuff is strictly 'need to know'."

Harry felt better, and then worse, and returned to the booth wondering exactly who Kelly thought might need to know.

"How'd you make out?" Nibber asked as he reamed a catsup bottle with his knife and gaped at Darlene, panting her way through the final verse of *Let's Get It On*.

"Okay, I guess." Harry didn't bother to explain, and the three ate quietly, listening to the next singer, Allie Knight, who was giving all she had to Madonna's *Like a Virgin* while four or five of her children frolicked and cheered in the back of the room. She was halfway through when Aidan Brown appeared in the doorway. He waited for her to wind up before looking for a seat. Nibber spotted him and waved, pointing to Debbie's empty place. Harry's stomach jumped. He was certain the trooper would mention something about them being at the O'Neil house last night.

Nibber caught on, but it was too late. "Might as well find out now, as later," he said, matter-of-factly.

Aidan, in plain clothes, sat down and shook hands all around. "Off duty," he said. "Working the day shift this week, but I pulled extra duty last night." He looked at Harry and Nibber. "You know why." Harry waited, certain the second shoe was about to drop, but it didn't. "Thought I'd stop by and see if poor Henry needs a ride," the trooper said. At the moment, Henry McLaughlin was on the singing stool, giving a slurry imitation of Willie Nelson's *Whiskey River*.

"You're so kind to that man," Diane said, nodding toward poor Henry. "How did you two ever become such good friends?" Harry knew she was trying to steer the conversation away from the murder.

Debbie came to the table and Aidan pointed at Nibber's longneck. Debbie nodded and headed off. "It's a long story," the trooper said.

"Tell us," Harry invited, even though he'd heard it all before.

"I was at the police station in Watford one cold night a couple of Januarys ago, doing some paperwork," Aidan began. "Poor Henry had been in several of the south end bars, and he stumbled into the station just after midnight, looking for a ride home. They couldn't lock him up because he hadn't done anything wrong, and they couldn't very well send him away because he would have frozen to death. I was coming back to Belfry anyway, so I offered him a ride."

"That was so nice of you." Diane kept focus.

Aidan shrugged. "You know Henry. A teddy bear when he's drinking. He'd been in the backs of cruisers before, but never in the front, and he amused himself by playing with the blue light. We were doing just fine until we got into town. I knew he lived on the East Road, but I wasn't sure exactly where."

"No driveway," Nibber interrupted. "Henry's been without a license so long that trees have grown where it used to be."

"Right," Aidan said, "because I went right past the place. Poor Henry never said a word, simply opened the door and jumped out." Diane put her hands to her mouth. "Thought he'd killed himself," Aidan went on, "but being in such a fluid state, he simply rolled a few times until he came to rest in a snow bank. He was already sitting up by the time I got to him. No broken bones, I checked, but it took some time to steer him into the house. I put him to bed, built a fire in the woodstove, and left. About two hours later, he called 911 to say his fire had gone out and he was hurting so bad that he couldn't get to the woodpile. I went back, stoked the fire, and tucked him in bed again. I thought that was the end of it, but at six he called again, to order breakfast."

Everybody roared, including Aidan. "I was off duty by that time," he said, "so I took Henry an Egg McMuffin and we had a long chat about life in general, and the real purpose of 911 in particular."

"What a terrific story," Diane said. "Like the old Chinese proverb: Save a man's life and you end up owning him." The thought seemed to unsettle Aidan, and he headed off to the bar to collect poor Henry.

It was 9:30, and no one was left in the singing line. As she always did when things began to slow down, Emily headed off to the table where Jeff Molony and the Deacon were huddled. Harry knew she was going to beg them to get up and sing. She hated having to tease them, but she knew it was the only way to clear the house.

The pair acknowledged a smattering of boos as they made their way to the stage. "Damn fools," Nibber said. "And what do you suppose they've been jawing about all night long?"

"God, probably," Diane suggested. "Or the dam. Or the murder. Or, most likely, all three."

The thought set Harry to fuming about the suitcase, and he raised his eyes to the ceiling where the spider was beginning to reconstruct her web. At least, he thought, we've held onto the money for twenty-four hours without being arrested, or murdered, or worse.

His reverie was broken by the startling disharmony of the Deacon and Molony singing *Go Tell It On The Mountain*. Instantly, patrons began to rummage around for their coats, not to head up any mountain, but to rush and pay their tabs. The place was nearly empty by the second verse. A minute later, smack in the middle of *When the Roll is Called up Yonder*, Durwood abruptly pulled the plug on the microphone and began packing up his things.

"This is good," Nibber said. "Once Debbie's finished clearing tables, we'll have our dam committee meeting." He winked at Harry. "And, whatever else it is we need to talk about."

8

Like the Knight's Store sign warning of falling ice, notices of Dam Committee meetings were widely ignored. To begin with, Nibber pestered to hold far more meetings than necessary, and the piled up announcements had become practically invisible. Moreover, after the long wrangling over whether or not to buy a new gate, most Belfry people were fed up with the whole dam business.

Harry worried that the slack attitude would lead to rejection of the spillway repair plan he was preparing for the coming Town Meeting, and he had pushed Nibber to step up the dam marketing campaign. Nibber responded by using a black felt marker to write **FINISH THE DAM THING** across the tops of the meeting notices that he tacked up everywhere along the full length of Main Street. Tonight, minutes before the ten o'clock scheduled meeting, it was plain to see the enhanced advertising hadn't done any good at all. The Sunrise was nearly empty.

"Don't feel badly," Nibber comforted as they sat around the vacated Gammon table under the wagon wheel. "We don't want hangers-on, anyway. We've got private business to take care of when we're done."

"Don't feel *bad*," Diane corrected as she glanced around the room. The only remaining patrons were

Molony and the Deacon, who, singing a capella and to themselves, had come to the end of *Good Night, God Bless You*. When they finally headed for the door, Molony suddenly changed direction and swerved toward the committee table, the gawky Deacon in his wake.

Molony wore a friendly grin, making Harry wonder if he had forgotten the morning confrontation at Knight's, or if the Deacon had put him in a forgiving mood. "Well now," Molony gushed when he pulled up, "it would appear we're about to have a meeting of the Dam Committee."

Harry gritted his teeth, forced a tiny smile. "It would appear."

"Bless you," Molony said in a syrupy voice, "but I'm afraid we can't stick around, and I was wondering if we might have a brief word, beforehand. You see, I'm trying to make arrangements for getting my boat docks put in, and I was hoping you people could tell me exactly when you plan to raise up the water. Don't want to have to move those heavy docks once they're in, you understand." The Deacon nodded an Amen.

Nibber had been lurking in the weeds. "Listen up, Bolony," he lunged. "God's the one who raises the water around here. You guys know him much better than we do. Why don't you ask him?"

The Deacon, eyes wide in astonishment, seemed to consider the suggestion when Molony bent down and sneered. "You're nothing but a contumelious clown."

"You, too!" Nibber shot back, perplexed.

The holy duo stalked off just as Debbie and Emily finished sitting breakfast plates on the last table. When Debbie plopped next to Nibber, Harry noticed the lettering on her new Dam Committee T-shirt was every bit as stretched as Nibber had hoped. Worse, dollops of spilled mustard clung to the two most prominent edges.

"My goodness," Nibber said, pointing at the twin blotches. "A mighty fine pair of nibs you've got there."

Diane shoved back from the table. Both she and her chair screeched. "Oh my God, Nibber!" she cried. "Have you no shame?"

Harry roared for the first time all night. Nibber's face was red. "The *mustard* nibs," he protested. "I was talking about the *mustard* nibs."

"Well, of course you were," Debbie soothed before promptly changing the subject. "Let's get this meeting on the road."

Harry called for order and asked for the secretary's report, nodding at Nibber, poised, pencil in hand. "All present. One guest." He glanced cautiously at the still-scowling Diane. "As for minutes of the last meeting, there ain't any."

Diane was set to correct him, but Harry cut her off. "Approved," he said. "And now, a report from the dam custodian." That was Nibber, too. Harry had appointed him soon after becoming head keeper. The job didn't pay much, but Nibber needed every cent he could get. A few in town noisily objected on grounds of nepotism and incompetence, and Harry went to Town Manager Susan Woods to defend Nibber's competence. He's a savvy mechanic, Harry told her, and besides, he was also the only one who knew how the new gate worked. Woods agreed, and passed over the charge of nepotism. Harry knew she would. Her brother was the cemetery sexton and her sister was town clerk. The flap blew over as quickly as it had blown in.

"I must tell you," Nibber said, launching into his report, "that new Tainter gate is slick as shit."

"Excuse me?" Diane interjected. "Will you be putting that in the annual report?" Harry ruled her out of order again.

"Tainter, now that's a real cute name." Debbie wasn't up on the jargon, and Nibber was eager to explain. "Named for the inventor," he said. "It's the curved steel gate. Tight seals on the sides, not like the old wooden one with its leaky slots. Goes up and down on an electric hoist. Easy as pie, like I said."

As he had done for the past six or so meetings, Nibber went on to explain that the fall lake drawdown brought the level of Grand Pond two feet below the spillway. Other than a bit of playful tinkering, he said, he hadn't changed the height of the gate all winter. "We bring the water down in October, before the fish spawn," he said, ogling Debbie. "Otherwise, we'd leave the eggs high and dry. And, of course, if we didn't take it down at all, we'd be washed out come spring."

Harry tried abbreviating. "Right now, Grand Pond and Finger Lake are below normal, but the runoff's about to start. Pretty soon she'll be up the banks, and we'll have to open the gate a bit so as not to overfeed Finger Lake and cause flooding on the Cebennek."

"Gee," Debbie said. "Seems like a very complicated business."

"Not really." Nibber was nonchalant. "Being a dam operator is a whole lot like being a dermatologist: if it's wet, you dry it, and if it's dry, you wet it."

Harry groaned. "That brings us to the central matter on the agenda," he said. "Town Meeting is coming, and if we don't get any more support than we've got right now, we won't have the money to fix the spillway."

Nibber resumed tutoring. "Here's the thing," he said, using his finger to draw a catsup map on a paper napkin. "Facing Finger Lake, the right side of the new dam abutment takes care of the near side of the spillway. That's all fine, but the problem is on the other side, along the shore, near Bolony's place. That wall is more than fifty years old. Made of rough sand from the stream bottom, and it's been eaten away over the years. Right now, you could put your whole arm in some of those cracks, and worse than that, water has gotten behind the wall, making it lean into the stream. Tips more every year. Pretty soon, gravity will take her over. Won't be long."

"So, what happens if it falls?" Debbie looked at Harry.

"Not a question of *if*," Harry said. "*When* it goes, the rush is going to gully-wash the entire shore. We'll have to open the gate to take off some pressure, but if we open it too much, we're sure to cause a flood down below."

"It seems to me it would be useful," Nibber said, looking at Harry, "if you would give us a good long-range forecast for the spring, just like you did for this winter."

"I did get that one right," Harry admitted, trying not to make too much of it. "And, if you don't mind me saying so, my short-term forecasts have been pretty good, too."

"Short forecasts are easy." Nibber was dismissive. "Nothin' to it."

Harry didn't argue. It was the seasonal predictions that were hard. He wouldn't have bothered to try, except that the former head keeper, Danny Gould, was uncanny in making long-term predictions, and Belfry people had come to expect it. Some people suspected the old man did it by reading pig spleens, but Harry had no immediate access to pigs, and wouldn't have known how to read their bloody spleens in any case. Instead, one day last fall he went to the magazine rack at Knight's, waited until he could be sure no one was watching, and took a quick peek at *The Old Farmer's Almanac*. After that, he went up and down Main Street boldly proclaiming that Maine was in for a wicked bad winter.

By mid-February, Harry's on-the-money prediction had brought him many fine compliments, and some, like Nibber, were already asking for a spring forecast.

"I'm not quite ready to make a prediction," he said. "First, we've got to get the town on our side on this spillway business." He turned to Nibber. "Any better ideas for a marketing campaign? The signs didn't work so good."

"Not so *well*," Diane said.

"No, they didn't," Nibber agreed. "And so far, only two of the five selectmen are behind us."

"Select *persons*." Diane took care of the two women on the board, and Harry rapped her out of order for the third time.

"These people don't want to spend a nickel," Harry moaned. "That's the problem with this town. Folks with the votes don't have any money, and folks with the money don't have any votes. The arrangement works out fine most of the time, like when flatlanders wanted to broaden Main Street and we stopped it, but in this case we could use some progressive thinking."

"You'd think Bolony would buy in," Nibber said. "When that wall comes down, he's gonna lose half his real estate in the first ten minutes."

"I spoke to Mr. Molony a couple of nights ago," Debbie said. "He's been dropping in at the Sunrise real often these days, trying to get me to sell him the farm."

"Warned you." Harry said. "Don't fall for it. That man wants *everybody* to sell out. He's after the O'Neil place, too. Won't stop until he's bought up everything in sight and sold the whole damn town to the flatlanders."

"I know all that," Debbie said, "but my point here is that, during these conversations, I found out he doesn't support the spillway. Says he trusts me, but you guys run the committee, and he says you two are troglodytes."

"For God's sake, what's *that*?" Nibber asked.

"Cavemen," Diane explained, looking at Harry. "The man has a point."

Harry ignored her. "He'll be sorry," he said. "Let's have a motion to adjourn."

"You got it," Debbie said. "I'm pooped."

Harry held up his hand. "Can't go anywhere yet. There's more."

* * * *

Emily had finished cleaning up in the kitchen and waved as she headed out the door. "You folks take as long as you like. Debbie's got a key. Lock up when you're done."

Harry listened for the sound of the latch, and then went to a window to look out. Satisfied there were no lurkers, he came back and hunched over the table. "This has to do with Doc O'Neil's murder," he said in a whisper, looking straight at Debbie.

"Cripes, one of you murdered him?"

"No, of course not, but it has to do with the murder, just the same."

"Spare me," she begged. "I've had my fill. That's all anybody talked about all night long. Mal was so busy flitting around she forgot to eat her rib eye. I saved it for Winston."

"Never mind crazy Mal," Harry said. "I don't suppose you heard any *sensible* theories on why Salome might have shot him?"

"Plenty of ideas, but none made any sense," Debbie said, pausing to think. "Doc was one real son-of-a-bitch, as you know."

"No clue there," Nibber shrugged. "If every son-of-a-bitch in Belfry got shot, the village would be half vacant. Besides, this meeting is not about the murder." He looked across the table at Debbie. "You'd better sit down," he said solemnly.

"I *am* sitting down," Debbie pointed out.

"Let me explain," Nibber began. "Winston was with Harry and I on the ridge last night."

"Winston was with Harry and *me*," Diane said, correcting.

"You weren't there," Nibber said, over-correcting.

Harry put his head in his hands. "That's not the point, anyway. Winston's got nothing to do with it."

"Wrong!" Nibber corrected again. "Winston was the one who found the suitcase."

Debbie's eyes darted back and forth, confused.

"Better let me tell this," Harry said. "We were up near the O'Neil house last night, not long after Doc bought it, and on the way home we found a suitcase full of money." Debbie cocked her head. "Half a million, Diane says, maybe more."

Debbie slid down in the booth, making her ponytail shoot straight in the air. "This is a joke, right?" She looked at Diane.

"Not a joke," Diane said. Debbie straightened up and launched a river of questions. Harry tried to answer.

"Whose money?"

"Doc's, we're pretty sure."

"Where is it?"

"In the rafters of my garage."

"Who knows about it?"

"Just us," Harry replied. "I hope."

"What are you going to do with it?"

"Haven't figured that out. Thought you could help."

"Help? How?"

"All good questions," Harry went on. "Let's take the first one. As I said, we're pretty sure the money belonged to Doc. Had to. It's the money he stole from the Black Wharf Gang before he went to jail. The papers had all of that. Must have hid it somewhere, went to get it after he got out of Ray Brook, and then brought it home."

Nibber poked at his last, cold catsup-soaked French fry. "We've pretty much decided not to give the money back to Doc, if that's what you're thinking."

Debbie grinned. "Oh, Nibber, you're a hoot."

Harry swallowed hard. "As a legal matter," he said, "I'm pretty sure it belongs to the Feds. They take confiscated drug money to run their own stings and pay for re-hab programs."

"Yes, but you'll notice they haven't yet confiscated this particular bunch of money," Nibber clarified.

"That's only because they can't find it," Harry said. "My point is that if we were to follow the letter of the law, we'd have to turn it in."

There was a long moment of silence before Diane finally spoke up, measuring her words. "I'm not at all sure it's a good idea to give the money to the government," she said. "It certainly wouldn't do Belfry a lick of good. The Feds don't run stings in Belfry, and they sure don't run any rehab programs here, either." She paused. "If they did, we'd enroll poor Henry."

Harry tried not to show his surprise. The woman who thought she ought to pay sales tax at yard sales seemed to be saying it was okay to keep the money. He decided to test the water. "Is there anybody who thinks we should give it up?"

Silence.

Finally, Nibber got slowly to his feet. "The way I see it," he said gravely, resting his knuckles on the table, "the money belongs to us." Harry put on a more worried look.

"See if this makes any sense," Nibber continued slowly. "Doc stole the money from the Black Wharf Gang, right?"

"Right." Harry agreed.

"The gang stole it from drug addicts up and down the east coast, right?"

"I suppose you could say."

"And, it's not much of a stretch to say the addicts got it from rich people."

"Well, yes ..." Harry felt a tiny bit stretched.

"So, exactly where do you think the rich people got it from?" Nibber surveyed the three faces. "From the rest of us, that's who."

"Oh, my," Debbie cooed. "Perfect logic."

"So," Diane said, "if we buy into that interesting line, I suppose we do keep it. But what would we do with it?

And, where do you all propose we keep it while we make up our minds?"

Nibber was beginning to think he had all the answers. "Why don't we just take it all down to our good friend Connie Bonney at The Old People's Bank, and ask her to put it in a savings account?"

"Nonsense," Diane said. "That much I know. Connie once told me that the law requires her to file a report on any transaction of more than $10,000."

"Well, then," Nibber did a quick calculation, "we'll just make fifty or so deposits of $9,999 each."

Harry plunked his forehead on the table. "Nope," Diane said, motioning for Nibber to sit down. "Bank tellers have an obligation to report *any* suspicious transaction. If you ever walked into People's with more than twenty dollars, Connie would first pass out, and when she came to, she'd call the FDIC right away."

"Maybe we could send Nibber on a plane to Switzerland and open an off-shore account." Debbie laughed at her own idea. So did Nibber.

"Let's never mind," Diane said. "Leave it in the garage."

"For now," Harry said.

"Okay," Harry summarized, "now, for the half-million dollar question. What will we do with it?"

Nibber was quick. "I'm so poor I eat my cereal with a fork to save milk."

"Me too," Debbie jumped in behind him. "Not *that* poor, but as you guys know, I'm about to lose my house."

After a long minute, Diane spoke up. "We could all use the money," she said. "That's for sure. And, some of us need it more than others, but I've got to say I wouldn't feel quite right about splitting it among ourselves. The only reason I went along with the idea of keeping it is because I got to thinking about how we might use that money in a better way than the government ever could. If we took it for ourselves, I just wouldn't feel comfortable. I really wouldn't."

Debbie cleared her throat. "She's right. It's dirty money. Sooner or later I'd feel rotten about it."

Harry watched Nibber, could see an argument coming. "Dirty money, clean money, who cares?" Nibber didn't disappoint. "I think I'd rather be an uncomfortable man with lots of money than a poor man with a good conscience."

It took a few seconds to figure out what Nibber had said, and in that time, Debbie gazed at him with mooneyes while patting his hand.

"Okay, fine," he said, not convincingly, "but it seems to me like a very unlikely outcome. If anybody tried putting it into a book, nobody would believe it."

"It's not so strange," Diane said, "considering the circumstances. Besides, we've got time to think about it. If we hold on, maybe we can find ways to use the money to help other people and pick things up for ourselves as well."

"I'd like that part of it," Nibber said, brightening. Debbie nodded.

"Sounds good to me," Harry summarized. "We'll become Belfry's good fairies, and along the way, we just might sprinkle a little magic dust on ourselves."

"Then it's done," Diane said, "and unless somebody objects, I'd say we begin things tomorrow morning by putting a thousand dollars in the special collection for renovations at the church."

"Church?" Nibber said. "I wasn't planning ..."

9

Harry rummaged through the top drawer of his dresser and pulled out his only necktie, a wrinkled blue affair with tiny, red dots. He hadn't worn it since he began his boycott of the Rev. Eugene Peppard, two years before. This morning he was set to break the strike, not for the spiritual lift but because he wanted to catch Kerri Woods and ask her about the mystery guests at Lake Lodge.

He stood in the mirror, pressing the tie against his chest with his hand, and began to wonder if his extended protest had done any good. His family had belonged to the Belfry Community Church for generations. He and Diane were married there and were regular followers during the long tenure of the Rev. Zachary Dyer. The old minister suited Belfry well, and under his leadership the open-minded and friendly congregation had grown to include not only a broad range of vanilla Protestants, but also a number of lapsed Catholics, several wayward Episcopalians, and even a few stray Jews.

Everybody got along and pitched in, but two years ago Dyer ran out of pastoral steam and retired, and a search committee headed by Deacon Jalbert recruited young Peppard away from the boisterous Glad Tidings Church in Watford. The flamboyant young minister hit the ground running, and without so much as a howdy-do, the week of his ordination he ordered the installation of a large changeable letter sign on the front lawn announcing the rebirth of the old church under the new name of Joyful Waters. That's when Harry quit. He was not only annoyed that Peppard hadn't consulted a soul on the change, but Harry also thought the new name was silly, especially the word "joyful," which matched neither Peppard's dogmatic preaching nor the declining mood of the parish members.

Harry wasn't alone in his outrage. In Belfry, where notions of change unfailingly met sudden and stiff objection, Peppard's edict didn't sit well at all, and Harry hoped for a time that the minister's brash action would be enough to send him packing. Instead, it was the members who began to walk away. The Jews left almost immediately, followed by all of the Unitarians, most of the Catholics, and several iffy Congregationalists. All that remained was a core of strict Baptists and Adventists, a handful of worried Methodists, and a dozen or so unattached folks like Harry, who clung to the comforting thought that the church would eventually outlive its pastor.

While he waited, Harry went on strike. He helped with weekday church projects, but he skipped Peppard's Sunday ranting. Diane carried on among the dwindling faithful and did her best to pull Harry back in line by pointing out that all preachers were flawed, even the broadminded and beloved pastor Dyer, who, she often pointed out, had built up the congregation even as he allowed the church building to fall to rack and ruin. On

that score, she was right. For years, he and Nibber had
joined most every crew that volunteered to patch things
up by jacking walls, replacing shingles, patching plaster,
restoring pews, and more.

For Harry, the first hopeful glimmer from Peppard
came when Diane returned from church one Sunday
about a year ago to say he had proclaimed that the
building did not match its joyful name, and that he was
immediately launching a campaign to raise money for a
full structural restoration. Although it was another
unilateral strike, in this case, Harry approved the target.

"Hurry up," Diane called upstairs, interrupting
Harry's musings. "If we're the last ones in, the general
shock of seeing you will upstage the minister."

Harry fussed with the knot of his tie for one last time
before heading downstairs where Diane waited by the
door. Winston was waiting, too, with a look of
disapproval on his face that grew more intense when he
discovered he wasn't going along. Harry hurried back
into the kitchen and tuned the radio to the dog's favorite
country western station, but Winston was still pouting
when he settled on the couch to wait it out.

"Don't answer the phone," Harry called back to him.
"It only confuses people."

They rode in silence until they crossed the bridge at
the dam and headed up the short rise to Joyful Waters.
"How's all the fundraising going?" Harry's question was
prompted by the sight of a blue tarp inelegantly spread
over the roof, covering a hole left by the recent removal
of the iconic belfry that had given the town its name.

"It's coming fine," Diane answered, obviously pleased by Harry's interest. "We'll make it. Peppard is very good at fund raising."

He's good at that, all right, Harry thought. The preacher had the money-making shtick all figured out, beginning with his timing of the late-May campaign kick-off the year before, precisely catching the arrival of flatlanders who were tired of being squeezed out of the limited seating and gathering their spiritual fodder while standing on the church lawn, drinking coffee and listening to Peppard's scolding through the open windows.

When they pulled into the church lot, Harry was further struck by the decay. The entire structure listed to the right, symbolically accurate, Harry thought, but placing the building in danger of collapse from the carpenter ants that had eaten away at the foundation timbers.

"Now, don't go getting upset with the reverend," Diane warned as they came up the walk. "We're here to listen to the word of God, not the minister."

"Can't be done. Peppard drowns God completely out," Harry sniffed as they neared the entrance where the old bronze bell rested with its clapper muffled on the ground, covered with a makeshift plywood tent. It had been down since last fall when Gus Gammon brought a cherry picker from the mill. Generations of bats in the belfry had caused so much decay that everybody agreed it had to come down before it fell on its own. They had been able to pop the bell out with no trouble, but the belfry clung stubbornly to the roof. Harry and Nibber helped to unfasten it and strap it on all four corners, but old man Gammon had barely began to swing it out over the front lawn when the entire structure exploded in a cloud of rotted wood and bat guano. Not a piece was worth saving, and the rescued bell now sat forlornly in the melting snow where Peppard had staked one of his quirky signs: **WRING OUT YOUR POCKETS & I'll RING OUT AGAIN.**

Harry groaned. It was going to be a long morning.

Just inside the tiny vestibule, Kerri Woods was seated at a card table under the empty bell rope hole, selling raffle tickets for a quilt made by the Crimson Crafters, a ladies group devoted to raising renovation money. "Mornin' Kerri," Harry said as he fished out his wallet to buy a dollar ticket.

"Morning to *you*." Harry caught the emphasis.

"Go ahead in," Harry said to Diane. "I'll be right along."

Kerri carefully put the quilt in a plastic bag. "We have to hurry," she said, adjusting her large red felt hat. "The service is about to begin."

"Can't miss that," Harry said cheerfully. "I'll be quick. I see you have guests at the Lodge, and I think I know one of them, the one in the white pickup, but I can't seem to place him."

Kerri wrinkled her brow. "Don't think so," she said doubtfully. "Neither one has ever been around these parts before. One of them came early Friday afternoon.

The other one, with the white pickup, arrived a few hours later."

"Just in case," Harry said, "do you remember their names?"

"Both paid cash," Kerri said," but of course I made them register. The man in the blue car is David Donihue. He stayed two nights. Left Saturday morning."

"And the white truck?"

"Still here," Kerry said. "Name's Lee Hemphill. Has a bad scar on his face. He's not actually rude, but he sure is close-mouthed. I asked lots of questions, and he dodged every one."

Aliases, Harry figured. Hemphill was probably the Nurse. The other guy, Donihue, was likely a federal agent.

"One more thing," Kerry added, folding the card table. "Although the car has Vermont plates, both men gave me Massachusetts addresses. Even so, I somehow don't think they know each other."

"That happens a lot in Massachusetts," Harry said, thinking that even though they didn't know each other, they were no doubt both in Belfry for the same reason.

* * * *

The sanctuary was only half filled, and most of the worshipers had taken the rear pews on both sides of the center aisle. Up front, the Deacon and his sidekick Molony held forth as unmoving ushers, smiling and waving back up the aisle as folks came in. Nibber had saved a pew on the right, in front of the Knight family, some of whose uncountable kids played with a bag of marbles while the rest held a frantic game of musical chairs along the two back rows.

Nibber stood up and explained he was holding the seat next to him on the aisle for Debbie. He motioned Harry and Diane in. It was an uphill climb. The outside building walls had been jacked up so many times without tending to the sagging center beams that the floor had taken on the shape of a v-hull boat.

Debbie arrived a minute before ten, out of breath. Nibber was delighted to see her, and the two snuck a quick hug just as Thelma McCracken sat down at the ancient upright under the pulpit and poised herself to pounce on the keys. She seemed a lot older and shorter than Harry had remembered, and he wondered if perhaps at the end of some not too distant recessional she was going to disappear altogether.

Thelma was not an especially good pianist, but even the few who could tell the difference blamed the bad music on the ancient piano that was sadly out of tune most of the year, except at Christmas. Worse, Diane recently reported that nowadays the poor woman's shortcomings were compounded by having to keep up with Peppard's modern music. She often lost her place mid-song, Diane said, resulting in a good many do-overs that extended the already well-stretched services.

At the stroke of ten, Thelma haltingly launched into Peppard's new theme song, *Living Water*, and at the beginning of verse two the rotund and bespectacled pastor made his grand entrance from behind the altar. He wore a flowing red robe and a broad snap-on white stole, embroidered with loons.

"Loons fit," Harry muttered.

"Shush!" Diane scowled.

After the sixth and final verse, Peppard swished to the lectern and promptly asked for a general bowing of heads for "a prayer of gratitude on the first anniversary of the double salvation of two of our most prominent leaders, Deacon Jalbert and Mr. Molony." Nibber looked at Harry, and the two were set to giggle when Diane glared a warning.

In the long moments of general silence, interrupted only by the occasional sound of a marble rolling on the seat of the pew in back, Harry recounted the double salvation story in his head. The year before, Molony and the Deacon had decided to take up scuba diving, but after a single lesson at the Watford YMCA, abruptly quit school. In early April, before the ice was completely out, they went into the open water at the dam outlet on Finger Lake, near Molony's place, hoping to see salmon bunching up in the fast water.

The mushy ice still hung on away from the shore, and when they ventured out to have a look, they spotted a giant pike and followed it for a minute or two before Molony came up to get his bearings. Although his oxygen tank was low, the Deacon strayed farther out, following the pike. When he finally tried to surface, he bumped his head under the ice, panicked, turned the wrong way, and headed out to sea. Molony went back down for a look and spotted his lost friend, arms flailing under the ice, twenty feet away. Molony gestured frantically to show the way, but he later said it was a full two minutes before the Deacon, wide eyed and gasping, made his way into the fresh air. The two sat on the bank for a time to catch their collective breath before they slogged in their heavy wetsuits up to Knight's Store to warm up. Allie Knight reported that Molony seemed the most terrified of the two, not so much by his near brush with death as by the Deacon's extreme reaction, weeping and carrying on about how he had been twice saved, by both his Lord and Savior and by Molony.

Afterward, there had been some local dispute over whether the Deacon had suffered brain damage from oxygen deprivation or if he had in fact run into Jesus under the ice, but everyone agreed that thereafter, he was immeasurably more pious and insufferable. Molony went along with the miracle theory, not so much because he believed it, Harry thought, but because it was good for business.

Following the memorial silence and the deep bows of the saved ushers, Peppard launched full bore into the regular service. He leaned heavily on the Book of Acts for the gospel, and for his sermon, went on in detail about the many responsibilities of sinners seeking redemption. Although the minister's thick glasses made it impossible to see his eyes, Harry was quite certain the terrorizing man was looking straight at him.

When the collection time neared, Diane began to fidget, and Harry knew why. She was ready to make the

first drop, and she was nervous. Earlier that morning he
had climbed over the garage and, without pulling out the
suitcase, raised the cover wide enough to pull a thousand
dollars from the pile in front that had been speared by
the electric drill. The total sum made a considerable
bundle, but Diane managed to get it all into a single,
unmarked Manila envelope that she now had jammed in
her pocketbook, sitting squarely on her lap.

"Don't you worry," Harry leaned over and said
softly. "We'll pull this off."

Peppard stood in the high pulpit and promised "a
wonderful   announcement"   following   the   dual
collections. As the Deacon and Molony began passing the
baskets up the aisles, Thelma led the congregation in *Lean
on Me*, which, Harry noticed, worshipers were actually
doing along the sloping pews.

Just as the renovation collection began, Harry
whispered to Nibber, seated on the aisle. "Distract him,"
he said, nodding at the advancing Deacon.

"Mornin' Mr. Jalbert," Nibber said when the Deacon
arrived. "Nice tie." Nibber then ceremoniously dropped
a quarter in the basket and then passed it along to
Debbie, who quickly sent it on to the trembling Diane.

The Deacon stared at Nibber and cocked his head
quizzically. He wasn't wearing a tie.

"Damn fool," he said after some hesitation, all the
while glaring into Nibber's grinning face. The exchange
took barely long enough for Diane to grasp the basket
with one hand, shove the fat envelope under a pile of
loose bills with the other, and quickly pass the basket on

to Harry, who in a single motion sent it behind him to the lively row of Knight kids.

The deed was done, and the Deacon and Molony marched solemnly to the front to present the week's revenue to Peppard, who blessed each basket separately before making his announcement.

"I want to tell you wonderful, generous people just exactly what your gifts have wrought," he began. "The renovation fund has at last reached more than $100,000." He paused for a smattering of applause, and then went on. "With another $75,000 or so, we can begin our renovations, but ..."

The "but" barely escaped his mouth when one of the Knight kids lost his grip on a marble, and it rapped sharply on the hard oak pew before it rumbled to the end and dropped with a smack into the sagging center aisle. Harry half stood to watch it pass. A real fine cat's eye rumbled down the keel of the aisle, steadily gaining speed before it struck the front of the altar platform and bounced a good foot in the air before it came to rest beneath the cross.

Peppard watched the entire episode in amazement and then looked up. "A sign," he said, spreading both arms over his head. "A sign from God that our prayers have been answered." He paused for effect. "And this wonderful sign has come from the mouth of a babe."

"Wasn't his mouth," Harry hissed. "It was his pocket. And he's not a 'babe,' either."

"Shush!"

Peppard went on. "For some time now, I've been thinking that a mere renovation is not good enough for this old church, or for you fine people, either, and I've been waiting for just such a sign to tell us that we can do much, much more." Dead silence. "I think we should continue with our extra collections until we have enough money to build an entirely new church, right here on this very holy spot." He either did not hear the gasps from the pews or he ignored them. "I'm calling a special meeting of church members for next Thursday night at eight o'clock," he said, "when we will decide whether we should simply patch things up around here or have ourselves a brand spanking new house of worship."

Gus Gammon had been dozing, but his wife had roused him for Peppard's proclamation, and the old man suddenly leaped to his feet. He was about to say something when his rouser grabbed his coattail and he sat down again. A number of others, including Nibber, raised their hands like schoolchildren, looked around sheepishly, and then pulled them down again. Harry looked at Diane and shook his head. If they hadn't been in church, there could have been an insurrection.

"He's got one great big fight on his hands," Harry hissed to Nibber as Thelma banged on the keys and led the riled-up congregation in a doubtful rendition of *Rock of Ages.*

10

Nibber glanced at each face around the table, waiting for full attention. When it was finally quiet, he began. "Salome was deranged and bound up," he said solemnly.

Diane jumped. "I believe you mean she was *arraigned* and bound *over*."

"Whatever." Nibber bristled at the interruption, and Harry put his head in his hands, peering through spread fingers. He'd known it was risky to assign Nibber as the lone court reporter for Salome's arraignment that morning, but there was no choice. He and Debbie had to work and Diane, who first agreed to go along, backed out at the last minute explaining that poor Salome was going to be embarrassed enough without having another familiar face in the courtroom. They'd all agreed to meet at the Sunrise for supper so Nibber could give a full report. He was off to a bad start.

"Okay," Harry said, staring coldly at Nibber, "Start again. Take it slow, and don't leave anything out."

"It was pretty simple, really," Nibber said, back on track. "The judge began by telling Salome she was being charged with the murder of Gregory O'Neil. That's Doc."

"We know," Harry said impatiently.

Nibber continued. "The district attorney, a jittery young fella named Webster Dean, got up said it was an open and shut deal. Salome had already confessed, several times in fact, and they had the gun with her prints on it. Simple as that."

"And?" Harry beckoned with his hands.

"Then Salome's lawyer, Tony Pasquale, came up and said there was no denying she'd killed, but it was in self defense. He said Doc came after her with a knife on the staircase, and she was afraid he was gonna kill her, and she had no choice but to shoot him. Pasquale asked the judge to dismiss the case, right then and there, but Dean jumped back up and said self-defense was a cockamamie idea that couldn't be proven because there were no witnesses. The judge must have agreed with Dean, because he said he wasn't changing the charge and then asked Salome how she wanted to plead." Nibber stopped and dragged an extra long French fry through a puddle of catsup on his plate.

"And?" Harry hunched his shoulders.

"Salome never said a word," Nibber explained, "but Pasquale said 'not guilty' for her, and when he did, she wiped a tear off her face. The judge said that was fine with him, and that she'd be bound up – or over – to superior court for trial."

"Is that it?" Diane asked.

"Oh, no," Nibber said, "Pasquale wasn't done. He strutted right back up to the bench and told the judge Salome would waive her right to a jury trial and wanted her case heard by a judge as soon as possible. Said there was no need to wait, that his case was ready. Prosecutor Dean thought a minute and then said that was all fine with him, and the judge agreed."

"All things considered, I'd say things went pretty well for poor Salome," Diane observed.

"You haven't heard the best part," Nibber went on. "After getting his way on those two things, Pasquale struts back and asks the judge if Salome could get out on bail while she waited for the trial. He said it was a special case because she needed to go home to Massachusetts to take care of her ailing mother."

"Massachusetts!" Harry sat straight up. "In Maine, they don't normally let people accused of murder out on the streets, much less out of state, and certainly not to go to Massachusetts."

"Or Rhode Island," Nibber added.

"Who said anything about Rhode Island?" Harry said. "Move on."

"Well, you should've heard Pasquale make his pitch," Nibber continued. "He went on about how Doc was a known criminal with a violent past and said Salome only killed him to keep from getting killed herself. He said she was not a threat to a soul, and she wouldn't hurt a flea. He called her 'sweet and innocent,' and a 'model citizen' and carried on like that."

"I think she's all of those good things," Diane said sympathetically.

"And apparently a damn fine shot, too," Harry chipped in.

"Anyway," Nibber grinned, "the judge said he didn't think he could let her out, but he called everybody up to the bench for a chat. I tried to listen, even moved up a few rows, but couldn't hear. Sorry."

Debbie patted Nibber's hand. "Now, don't you be sorry. You did just fine."

"Thanks," Nibber squeezed her hand and glanced at Harry. "I think I did."

Harry ruined the sweet moment. "So what happened then?"

"After a few minutes, the judge broke it up and said because of special circumstances having to do with Salome's need to care for her sick mother, he'd set bail at five hundred thousand dollars and make arrangements for Salome to return to Chelsea while she waited for trial."

"She must have put up the house on the shore," Harry said. "All paid for. Not a problem."

"Very unusual arrangement," Diane said, "but I'm glad for her. Her mother really is quite sick, you know."

"Maybe," Harry said, "but up to now she's managed to care for her only on weekends, and not every weekend, either."

"None of that came up," Nibber said.

"We did learn a couple of things," Harry said when Nibber had finished. "Pasquale claims Doc came after Salome with a knife and they met on the staircase. That much we didn't know, but still, the whole thing doesn't add up. Doc's been gone three years. Why the devil would he come home one fine day and try to kill his wife?" Harry thought some more. "And if she didn't think he was coming home until Saturday, how come she was ready and waiting with a loaded .357 on Friday night?"

"All good questions," Diane admitted, "and there'll be answers, don't you worry."

Harry fretted anyway. "You think she might be covering for somebody?"

"Could be the Nurse," Nibber suggested. "Maybe she was in bed with him. You know, like in bed in business and in bed in bed."

"I know what you mean," Harry said, "and we can't rule it out. At the same time, she might be covering for somebody else, somebody we don't even know, like the guy with the rental car. We're only guessing he's a cop."

"Or maybe Peppard," Nibber added. "He told us the day we took down the belfry that Doc was an evil man, and we all know how hard Peppard works to stamp out evil."

Diane was flabbergasted. "Oh, Nibber, for the love of Pete, you have a wild imagination. And by the way, was the good reverend even in court this morning?"

"Nope," Nibber said, "but his lieutenant, the Deacon, was there. Right up front."

"Who else?" Diane wanted to know.

"A couple of reporters," Nibber said, "but not many Belfry folks. There was Aidan Brown and Kelly Hallowell of course, officers of the law, and Henry McLaughlin was in the back. I don't know why he came. He didn't pay any attention. Maybe Trooper Brown brought him for an outing."

"That was really nice of Aidan," Diane said. "Henry must have liked it."

"Oh, I'm sure he did," Harry said. "He's right at home in a courthouse."

"And, oh yes," Nibber added, "I almost forgot. Mal Grandbush was there. Sitting way up front when I got there. In fact, she was at the table where Salome and Pasquale were supposed to sit. They made her move when things got started."

"Well thanks, Nibber," Harry said, grateful the report had ended. "That wasn't so bad after all."

Debbie smiled approvingly and popped up to take care of a young woman, picking up take-out at the cash register, carrying a baby in a sling. Diane followed Debbie to have a closer look, and Harry felt a sudden twinge as he watched her, silly talking, kissing and cooing. He knew what she was thinking.

Nibber caught on. "How's that all going?" he asked Harry.

"It's not," Harry replied.

"Don't give up," Nibber said. "Can't hurt to keep trying."

When all four were settled in again, Nibber announced he had more to report. "You're gonna like this part," he said. "After the hearing, when everybody was about to leave, Kelly Hallowell came over and said Salome wanted to talk with me."

"You actually talked with her?" Diane was surprised.

"I did," Nibber said. "I was afraid she might be all in a puddle because of the mess she's in, but she wasn't. Cool as a cuke. She gave me a big hug and said I looked real nice." He turned to look at Debbie. "I'd shaved and combed my hair good, and I had on a real shirt, you know, with buttons." Debbie smiled adoringly.

Harry pressed on. "What'd she want?"

"She asked if I'd go over to the house, turn off the water and the heat and stuff like that. I have the key, you know. I said I would. Then, as I was about to leave, she called me back and whispered in my ear. Asked if I would mind cleaning up the mess."

"The mess?" Debbie didn't get it.

"The stairway," Nibber explained, "where Doc got it."

"Goodness," Debbie said, "that *would* be a mess, now wouldn't it?"

"Are you sure it was okay for you to go over there?" Harry was on a different track.

"Oh yes," Nibber replied. "I'm not silly. I asked Aidan and Aidan asked the DA. The house is not a crime scene anymore. The state boys have taken all the pictures and removed all the evidence they need. The DA said it was okay and as a matter of fact, I stopped by the O'Neils' on my way over here."

"You should have waited for me," Harry was emphatic.

"Turns out you're right," Nibber grimaced. "I ended up not turning anything off because I could see right away I was gonna need a lot of hot water. There's blood all over the landing and, worse than that, little tiny pieces of Doc all over the wall."

"Yuk!" Debbie said, closing her eyes.

Nibber patted her hand and turned to Harry. "I ripped off the sheetrock at the foot of the stair landing. Had to come out. Big hole. Wall splattered with blood. Turns out the bullet hit square on the front edge of a two-by-four stud. The cops had dug out the slug, but the hole went deep. I've seen that stuff on TV, so I thought I'd try a little experimenting of my own. Took the handle off the fireplace poker and stuck the end in the bullet hole."

"And?" Harry asked.

"Well, it's funny," Nibber said, "they'd fussed in the hole to get the bullet out, but when I stuck the poker in as far as it would go, the thing seemed to aim straight up the stairs."

"Well, of course it did," Harry said. "She was standing at the top of the stairs when she shot him."

"Yes," Nibber agreed, "but even so, from the slant of the poker she must have been holding the gun way over her head."

"Maybe you got it wrong," Diane said.

"Or maybe the bullet got off course when it went through Doc's head," Harry speculated.

Debbie asked if anybody wanted anything to eat.

"Meatloaf," Nibber said.

"The day's soup," Harry said. "And get Nibber some catsup. His bottle's half empty."

"Nibber's is half *full*," Diane said. "Yours is half empty. Soup for me, too."

Debbie hurried off to put in the order, and Harry changed the subject. "While we're here," he said, "we ought to try to figure out how we can stop the lunatic

Peppard from carrying out his plan to build a whole new church."

"We've just got to save it," Diane agreed. "Needs some fixing, but we can't let him replace the whole thing."

Harry looked around. Debbie had returned to the table, and except for Emily Boulette, busy in the kitchen, the place was empty. "If we'd known Peppard had such nutty ideas," he said quietly, "we never would have put a thousand dollars in the basket last Sunday. It's only going to encourage him in his foolishness."

"The problem is," Nibber said, "the only church members left are the ones who will go along with Peppard. I'd say we're sunk."

"Maybe not," Diane said. "There are a couple of things we can do. First, we get hold of as many old-timers as we can, and tell them to attend the special meeting Thursday night."

"We already know Gus Gammon and his family don't want a new church," Harry offered. "The old man had a fit when Peppard announced his crazy idea. Afterward, when we were outside, Gus reminded me that the church is the oldest building in town, the only one left from the early days. He isn't about to give up without a fight. Neither will the Knights. John told me yesterday."

"Cripes, come to think of it, if they allow the Knight kids to vote," Nibber grinned, "we're home."

Diane leaned over the table. "Okay, so we'll get a crowd, but I have another idea I think might cinch it." Harry cocked his head; she hadn't told him. "You might not go along with this," she said, "but if I must say so myself, I think it's terrific." All three listened carefully as she spelled it out. When she had finished, Nibber and Debbie were grinning. Harry looked doubtful, but after a minute or two, nodded his head.

"Fine with me," he said.

11

Diane planned an early supper, to be ready for the eight o'clock meeting at Joyful Waters, and she was at work in the kitchen when suddenly there was a loud knock. "Who's that tap, tap, tapping at my door?" she asked.

Harry was watching the evening news with Winston, and caught on right away. "Lenore, maybe?" She had quoted Poe before.

"Don't be silly," she said. "It's not midnight; it's suppertime. It's got to be Nibber."

Winston spun his paws on the wood floor and raced to the door to greet his friend, swiping his gloves before the two paraded around the kitchen, talking gibberish. "Enough!" Diane barked when they upset a chair and sent it clattering across the floor.

Winston slunk off disgustedly, and Nibber settled into his usual seat at the table, breathing heavily. "Am I interrupting?"

"You do have a way of interrupting at the most personal moments," Harry sputtered, "including mealtimes."

Diane smiled, looked at Nibber. "Someone gave Harry a pail of smelts at the mill today," she said. "Want some?"

"Sure," he said, even as Diane began setting another place. "Golden brown. Extra salt. Don't have to clean 'em, but take the heads off, if you don't mind."

Diane rolled her eyes, and Nibber's face grew serious. "Gotta have another meeting of the Dam Committee," he declared. "Right away."

"For cripe's sake, why?" Harry asked. "We just had one."

"Got a call from the state boys this afternoon," Nibber explained. "The SWE is way high."

"Swe?" Diane looked at Harry.

"Snow-to-water," he said, turning to Nibber. "How high?"

"Four feet of snow pack, and some of it is forty percent water. The melt could raise the ponds six or eight inches higher than we figured."

"We'll meet later at the dam, on the way to the special church meeting," Harry said. "It won't take long. You pick up Debbie." Nibber nodded eagerly.

Diane put the fried smelts on the table, and Nibber grabbed a fistful for his plate, covering them with catsup. Diane turned up her nose. "Holds the salt," he explained.

Harry's mind was on the dam. "The solution will be to raise the Grand Pond gate," he said, "but it's gonna be tricky this time of year."

Nibber's eyes brightened. "Taking the water down under the ice will be fun," he said. "The fishermen will have a fit."

* * * *

After supper, Nibber hurried off to get Debbie, and the two were already on the catwalk when Harry and Diane pulled into the small turnout near the dam. Nibber was bending over the rail, pointing into the frothy water, explaining something to Debbie, who clung to every word.

"Wait 'til you see what Nibber's done," Debbie exclaimed when Harry and Diane began to inch out over the steel walk.

"Good Lord, what?" Harry asked nervously.

"Look there." She pointed to a large steel box attached to the dam abutment, hanging out over the spillway.

"What's that?" Harry inquired, clutching the neck of his jacket.   "Toolbox," Nibber said proudly.

"For what?"

"Tools."

"What tools?"

"Sledge hammer, monkey wrench, screw drivers, duct tape. Stuff like that. It'll save me running back and forth to the truck." Nibber looked at the frowning Harry. "And don't you worry about a thing. The box is bolted to the new dam wall, has a padlock, and the catwalk is always chained."

"Damn fool!" Harry shook his head. Nibber looked hurt.

"He calls you a damn fool because he loves you," Diane soothed. "Go on now. Have your committee meeting. It's cold out here."

"Simple enough," Harry said, pointing to the gauge on the Grand Pond side of the dam. "She's been down twenty inches all winter, but we can go down another few inches without much trouble at all."

"Doesn't seem like much of a difference," Debbie interjected.

"Two or three inches over nine thousand acres is a heck of a lot of water." Nibber waved his arms out over Grand Pond.

"It'll take days," Harry said. "Let's start."

Nibber opened the control box and pressed the button to raise the gate. "This is gonna scare the bejesus out of a few people," he said.

"How's that?" Debbie didn't understand.

"When the water goes down, the ice will fracture," Nibber explained. "Sounds like cannon. Ridges form where the ice breaks and overlaps, and then the water rushes in and freezes over the skids of any fishing shacks that happen to be nearby." He watched the slowly rising gate, his finger on the button. "That's the part that tickles Harry," he said. "The fishermen will have to chop out their skids in order to get their shacks off the ice by the end of March."

"Yes, indeed," Harry grinned. "Nobody can say this job doesn't have its rewards."

"You have a weird sense of humor," Diane remarked as they followed Nibber's smoking truck up the road to Falling Waters.

"Comes from hanging out with him," Harry explained as they both drove past the already-filled church parking lot and found parking places along the side of the road.

On the walk back, it was easy enough to see that Peppard's proposal had raised a crowd, and from the latest version of the front lawn movable letter sign it was apparent that the minister was hard at work advertising his case:

ALL NEW
NO GLUE
CAN DO

"Politics," Harry grumped. "Raw politics."

"Never mind." Diane turned to Nibber. "You ready to do your thing?"

"Guess so."

The assembly was much bigger than Sunday's, and tonight even the front rows were mostly filled. Harry craned his neck to do a rough count. The minister's allies were mostly bunched in the front – the Deacon, Molony, postmaster Hummer and a number of the newcomers who had followed Peppard from Glad Tidings in Watford. Toward the back were several old-timers Harry hoped would stand up for renovation. Scott Gammon and John and Allie Knight were there with their families. Kerri Woods and the old dam keeper Danny Gould were in the middle along with Mal Grandbush, who had been in a tizzy all week, polling and lobbying up and down Main Street. Emily Boulette had closed the Sunrise early and brought her cook, Brendan Pearl. Down front, in the midst of the enemy, Harry recognized Henry

McLaughlin and the shrinking pianist, Thelma McCracken.

"About even, I'd say," Henry muttered to Diane.

Peppard appeared at the stroke of eight and walked off the altar platform to a microphone set up on the sloping floor in front of the pews. He was in street clothes, and the knot of his necktie jacked up one side of his collar. A shirt flap hung over the belt of his rumpled trousers.

"Before we begin," Peppard said, already beginning, "I must announce that I have received yet another miraculous sign." There was a smattering of loud groans. "When we counted the special collection after last Sunday's service," he said, "we found a plain brown envelope." Harry could hear Diane suck in her breath. "Believe it or not," Peppard went on, "inside we found almost a thousand dollars in cash."

Harry stiffened. *Almost*? It was *exactly* a thousand dollars. He'd counted it, three times.

Peppard seemed to relish the surprise. "The instant I saw all that money," he said with a flourish, "I was struck by two very strong feelings – gratitude and embarrassment – both at the same time. Does anybody know how that feels?"

It was a rhetorical question, but Nibber popped up anyway. "Maybe like how you feel when somebody tells you your fly is unzipped?"

Peppard was at first dumbstruck, then looked down and quickly sidestepped his way back up behind the pulpit. About half the crowd broke into giggles, a fair indicator to Harry of where things were going.

"You're not helping," Diane hissed in Nibber's ear.

"Sorry." Nibber stifled a giggle of his own.

The agile pastor recovered and went on. "Thank you for that, Mr. Nabroski," he said, pretending. "Truth is, I meant I was entirely grateful for such a large contribution made in a most unselfish sort of way." He waved his hands over the gathering. "And at the same time, I was a little embarrassed to think there are not more people willing to dig so deeply for such a worthy cause."

Peppard moved promptly to take advantage of both the guilt trip and his hiding place, and he read from Saint Matthew's account of the Sermon on the Mount, making a special point of the blessings that would come to those who gave alms without sounding trumpets.

"No need to come back on Sunday," Harry whispered to Diane. "We're covered, and it's only Thursday."

"Shush!"

When he finished preaching, Peppard ventured back to his earlier spot on the floor and opened the business session. "As I reported on Sunday," he said, "we have already collected more than a hundred thousand dollars for church improvements, $101,678 to be exact." Harry admitted to himself that it was a remarkable sum after only a year of second collections.

"Here's what I'm thinking," Peppard said. "Thanks to the lumber discounts offered by brother Gammon, we already have enough money for the necessary materials.

It would take another eighty or so thousand to pay for the labor, and we could begin renovations."

The minister wiped his glasses on his shirttail, put them back on, and gazed intently into the faces of his flock as he neared the punch line. "However, as you now know, I've seen a far brighter light, and I have come to realize it would take only a year or so longer to raise enough money to build an entirely new and wonderful tabernacle on these same hallowed grounds."

He'd pulled the trigger, and it was time for everybody to weigh in. Gus Gammon was first. He rose slowly to his feet and looked down at a sheet of paper in his hand. "This church was built by our first settlers," he said, "more than a hundred and fifty years ago. They raised the money for the bell, had it shipped from Boston, and put it in the belfry that gave this town its name."

The place grew quiet as Gammon went on with his lesson. "This here is the oldest building in town, and it has seen a lot of history." He looked at his notes. "From the building of the dam that doubled the size of Grand Pond in a single summer; through the days of the railroad, when summer tourists came by the trainload; through the end of the Industrial Revolution, when local people began to sell off to folks from away, and the fences went up." He'd covered a century in a single sentence. "That brings us to today," he wound up, "when we are faced with deciding whether to ignore our past or preserve it. I hope you will all agree to save it." With a smattering of applause, the old man sat down.

Up front, the Deacon was ready, and he towered to his astonishing full height. "I, for one, have great fondness for our past," he intoned, "but we all know the current situation calls for both a reality check and a little imagination." Harry looked at Nibber, who arched his eyebrows. The Deacon went on. "The reality is that this place is beyond repair and we need to muster our imagination to envision what a glorious new church we could have for ourselves."

"Bullshit!" The startling comment came from somewhere near the Deacon, and Harry turned his head to see. It was poor Henry McLaughlin.

"Must have pre-loaded," Nibber whispered as Peppard shot Henry a stern look and Gammon got back on his feet. "Listen to me," he said, looking directly at the Deacon. "We've seen those new, ready-built churches. They're poppin' up everywhere. They're nothin' but a couple of vinyl-covered doublewides pushed together, with skinny aluminum steeples that don't fit the buildings they sit on. Nothin' very realistic or imaginative about any of that."

The Deacon opened his mouth to rebut, but nothing came out. Danny Gould filled the gap. "I know a bit about construction," the retired dam custodian said, without getting up, "and you can't put a heavy bell on top of a double-wide. The whole place would fall down."

Molony jumped up beside the still-standing Deacon. "Who said we planned to use double-wides?" he asked. "And who said what we intend to do with the bell? This is ridiculous, a big kafuffle over nothing."

Harry shot a quizzical look at Diane, who shrugged.

"What's ridiculous is the idea of building a whole new church in the first place." The voice came again from poor Henry, expanding upon his earlier thought.

Next up was an alumnus from Glad Tidings. Harry didn't know him. The man moved into the center aisle and pointed to the slanting floor. Heads looked down. "Take a good look," the man said. "Beyond repair." Then he shot his arms to the ceiling where sections of the blue tarp showed through the hole where the belfry had been. Heads looked up. "A disaster," he said.

Finally, the man waved a hand toward the single stained glass window, behind the altar. Heads turned ahead. It was a depiction of the Sermon on the Mount, and the settling front wall had cracked one of the glass pieces in a line that went straight through Moses' 'Thou Shall Not Steal' tablet. "You've got to admit," the man said in a satisfied way, "this place is hopeless."

Harry steamed. He'd promised himself he wouldn't say a word, but he couldn't help it. He jumped to his feet and spoke without waiting for Peppard to call on him. "All of this can be fixed," he sputtered, shaking his finger toward the stained glass window, "and don't forget, Moses was once a basket case, too." Almost everybody laughed, and Harry sat down, feeling smug.

The debate raged for more than an hour, one side then the other. Things seemed to be going badly for the renovators until Peppard dragged his feet on estimating the cost of a whole new church, and Harry began to think maybe some of the minister's supporters were beginning to stray, put off, no doubt, by the prospect of endless extra collections.

Finally, Molony tried ending the debate. "It's time for a vote," he said, bowing his head here and there around the room. "We've had quite enough tergiversation."

"Dubbing around," Diane whispered along the pew.

Molony continued. "I move that we make plans for an entirely new church building, and that we continue the current campaign until we raise the full amount, whatever it is."

"Second," said the obedient Deacon.

"Further discussion?" Peppard asked.

Harry looked at Nibber, who promptly raised his hand.

"Mr. Nabroski?" Peppard was impatient.

Nibber stood at his place. "The way I see it," he said, "this is a lot like having a favorite pair of old shoes that needs new soles and stitching." Harry knew where Nibber was headed. They'd all agreed at the Sunrise. What surprised him was that Nibber had prepared a sermon on shoes.

"Tonight we have the same choices we do when our shoes wear out," Nibber went on. "We can fix the old ones or buy new ones. It's that simple. And I can tell you from experience that whenever I've given up on my old shoes and bought new ones, they look good but they hurt my feet, and they squeak."

Harry was proud. The analogy was imperfect, but Nibber rarely spoke in public and never about anything as profound as old shoes.

When Nibber's homily ended, he paused and looked straight at the new-church proponents in the front. "As you can tell," he said, "I have strong feelings about all of this, and I've given it plenty of thought. I know a lot about this old church, every timber and every board and shingle, and I know it can be saved. I also know we can't wait long. We already have enough money for the materials, and I'm here to tell you that I am willing to contribute the labor. No charge. My friends will help me when they can."

Peppard looked pleadingly at the Deacon, then Molony, and finally Nibber, who addressed him directly. "My dear reverend," he said politely, "we can begin the job next week if you like. I promise we'll be done by fall."

Nobody said a word until Thelma McCracken stood up in front and rhythmically began to slap her hymnal with her tiny white gloves – clap, clap, clap. In a second or two she was joined by Scott Gammon, who pounded his big hands on the back of the pew in front. The Knight kids, inspired by the commotion, began to whoop it up in the back row, and before long, everybody was shouting and clapping except for the Deacon, Molony and a few others who sat, shoulders sloping, glumly looking straight ahead.

When the cheering stopped, Peppard recognized the Deacon, who spoke slowly and carefully. "Well, now," he drooled, "that's a very nice offer, Mr. Nabroski." The Deacon never called him 'mister.' "However, we must think very carefully before we accept your kind and generous offer. You have lots of other jobs to do, and we all know how hard you work to make a living. To be honest, I really don't see how you are going to be able to fit in the reconstruction of an entire church."

Nibber was calm. "I make my own schedule," he said. "I said I can do it, and I will."

"Yes," the Deacon said, "but you have to understand that some of us here have serious fiduciary responsibilities to Joyful Waters Church."

"He thinks *he's* got fiduciary responsibilities," Harry whispered in Diane's ear. "He ought to have the damned suitcase."

"Shush!"

Old man Gammon didn't wait to be recognized. "Come now," he said, "we all know Nibber. He and his father never cheated a soul and they finished every job they ever started. We're lucky to have his offer. Let's just say 'thank you' and be done with it."

Peppard was licked, and he knew it. The Deacon and Molony seemed stunned when the minister threw in the towel. "We don't need a vote," he said. "It's settled."

Everyone in the sanctuary sat quietly, digesting what had taken place. Again, it was tiny Thelma who broke the spell when she went to the old spinet and banged out *Onward Christian Soldiers* without a hitch.

As folks made their way to the door, many bunched around Nibber, swamping him with handshakes and slaps on the back. Diane watched with tears in her eyes and smiled as Debbie planted a kiss on Nibber's cheek.

Peppard, who normally had clear sailing down the aisle to the vestibule, had to fight his way to his customary greeting spot by the door. He arrived barely ahead of Nibber and his entourage, and Harry watched as Nibber shook the pastor's hand, then steered him off to a corner where the two stood quietly talking for a minute or more.

"What was that all about?" Harry asked when they were finally outside.

"Health insurance," Nibber said.

"Health insurance?"

Nibber looked around to make sure no one could hear. "You see, our plan calls for me to take my wages out of the suitcase. That doesn't include health insurance, or does it?"

"No." Harry shook his head. "No insurance, no taxes, no Social Security and no worker's comp. Cash. That's it. In small bills."

"Fair enough," Nibber agreed. "Peppard said he couldn't give me health coverage, but said he would make sure the Joyful Waters insurance includes liability, in case I fall off the roof."

"I'm surprised Peppard even talked to you," Harry said.

"*You're* surprised? I was stunned. In fact, he was most gracious. Told me he'd misread the signs. Said he was delighted by my offer, even offered to help."

12

The birds were chirping hopefully, and the morning air was filled with smells of thawing ground and budding trees. Patches of new grass were spreading in the wake of the retreating snowdrifts, and tiny crocuses showed their yellow heads near the foundations along the road. It was the third Saturday of March, Town Meeting day, a certain mark of spring.

Harry wasn't taken in by the promising signs, and as he slowed the truck near the crosswalk at Knight's Store, he felt the need to adjust the mood. "We'll be having more snow," he announced to Diane. "Plenty of it." She ignored him and turned to wind down the window and watch as a cheerful crowd of locals came from every direction, toting picnic baskets and towing children. The entire village seemed to be headed for the Belfry Grange, eager for the year's first chance to catch up on gossip, ventilate stored gripes, and take in old-time democracy at its raw and raucous best.

Despite his gloomy prediction, Harry was in a generally optimistic mood until they crossed over the bridge by the dam, where he was reminded that the otherwise sensible scheme of one man, one vote would probably backfire later in the day, when he asked for money to repair the spillway. Belfry people didn't like to spend money, and their tight-fisted approach was never more in evidence than at Town Meeting.

Harry parked across the road in the church lot, and as they tiptoed over the muddy lawn, he pointed to Peppard's ever changing sign, revised for the occasion with arrows pointing to Joyful Waters and the Grange across the way:

PREPARE YOURSELF
FOR DEATH →
← AND TAXES

Diane said the sign was evidence that the good pastor had recovered from his resounding defeat at the hands of his flock two nights before. "He's really quite a good sport," she said, nodding at the sign.

"A political realist, that's what," Harry countered firmly as they jostled their way through the double doors of the Grange and were instantly greeted by a blast of hot air. It was the same every year. The dutiful custodian would forget both the certainty of rising daytime temperatures and the body heat generated by a crowd, and build a raging fire in the iron woodstove up front. This morning, except for the vacant arc of chairs in front of the cherry-red potbelly, most every seat was taken, and the room was filled with smells of damp wool and soggy leather boots, mixed with an occasional whiff of flannel Long Johns, sewn on since November.

Nibber had arrived early and was using copies of the *Belfry Annual Report* to save several places on a long wooden bench under the windows along the wall. "Best seats in the house," he greeted them. "Just don't look at the murals."

Harry didn't need a warning. Sometime in the 1950s, an art class at the Belfry Elementary School had painted the scenes, six in all, between the tall windows on both sides of the room. The Grange Master saw the project as a free paint job, and the art teacher was only too eager to display the talents of her budding artists. It might have worked out, but trouble began when the Belfry Business Group insisted that all of the murals be scenes of the lakes, at once presenting the awkward challenge of drawing horizontal ideas in vertical spaces. The result was a great deal of water, with waves of all sizes heading in wildly different directions and painted in the full blue palette, from tame azure to angry Prussian. Taken as a whole, Nibber said the collection made him seasick.

This morning, as Harry gazed separately at the three scenes on the opposite wall, it occurred to him that the greatest planning failure of the long-ago project was that no one had taken into account the remarkable durability of acrylic paint. The six water-filled displays were every bit as bright and alarming as the day they were unveiled, and they now stood as the only surfaces of the entire hall, inside or out, that weren't chipping paint. The sharp contrast cried out as proof that the Grange was on its last legs, barely kept alive, Harry knew, by a handful of determined old farmers who tried their best to make ends meet by renting out the hall for wedding receptions, snowmobile club meetings, potluck suppers, and Watford College fraternity initiations.

Old man Gammon once explained to Harry that in the beginning, when the lines between church and state were muddy like the season, Town Meeting was held at the community church. Later, after lawmakers gave the First Amendment a closer read, the mixing was forbidden, but even so, it took another twenty years before the people of Belfry got around to moving the proceedings across the road. These days, fraternity initiations were about as exciting as the old Grange ever got, and Harry wondered if maybe the time was not far off when the place would fall to ruin, and Town Meeting would have to be moved again.

Harry's survey of the shabbiness was interrupted when Town Manager Susan Woods walked onto the low stage and went to a table set in the gap of the faded and tattered blue velvet curtain. The curtain had come off the trolley in the middle of some long ago comedy performance by the Odd Fellows and the Daughters of Rebekah, and hadn't moved since. As she took her seat, Woods was careful not to touch the velvet and get the dust onto her new blue suit.

She rapped the gavel and promptly called for nominations for a moderator. Someone up back yelled "Sandy Gemery," and without waiting, she banged the hammer and declared it done. The stone-faced Gemery had been the automatic choice as moderator for many years. Not only did he have a fair grasp of *Roberts Rules of Order*, but the retired Watford High civics teacher also had valuable experience in the business of bringing group order out of general chaos.

Gemery thanked the assembly and gave the floor back to Woods, who began her report by assuring everyone that despite the multiple arrests of poachers and the recent murder of Doc O'Neil, the town's crime rate was still moderate. At the same time, she noted an upturn in suspicious activity reports from the Sheriff's Department and expressed regret that the number of dogs in the village continued to outnumber the number of dog licenses being issued. Diane penciled a note to remember to get a tag for Winston.

The manager then moved on to report results of the secret balloting, conducted at Town Hall the day before. The town budget had been approved, she said, but by only a few votes. She then launched into a lecture about the responsibility of citizens to be informed of the issues and went on to say that just because people were fed up with property taxes, it was no excuse to make an automatic 'X' in the 'no' box when voting on the budget.

Harry glanced at Nibber, who cupped his hands over his mouth and stuck out his tongue, revealing how he had voted the day before. Nibber made no bones about liking the earlier days when budget matters were thrashed out at Town Meeting, but others had successfully argued that the issues were too complex for once-a-year voters to absorb, and it was much better to leave the messy budget to the selectpersons, vote the whole thing up or down behind the curtain, and thereby free up Town Meeting for more digestible and entertaining matters.

Woods continued with a report of new town appointments, all renewals, including her sister Ruth as town clerk and her brother Digger in multiple posts as cemetery sexton, tree warden, and animal control officer. She had no more than finished when brother Digger asked for the floor.

"I am gravely worried," he said without appreciating his pun, "if Belfry people keep dying at the present rate, we're gonna run out of places to put 'em." A man of few words, he sat down abruptly, leaving his dire prediction hanging in the warm, stale air.

"I thought everybody died at the same rate," Nibber whispered to Diane. "One per person."

"Shush!"

Momentarily put off stride, Gemery recovered to say he was sure the Board would appoint a special committee to look into the evaporating real estate. Woods nodded and went on to announce the re-election of Bo Chilton as road commissioner. Although the popular Chilton was never opposed, the crowd roared its approval just the same.

When the cheering stopped, Gemery recognized a man in the back who was careful to explain that he meant no criticism of Bo, but he'd been watching out his window one morning last January when the town plow sent a huge drift into his mailbox, knocking it a kilter. An hour later, he said, the mailman misjudged the new positioning of the box and flattened it with his truck.

"The mailman left a note," the man said. "I thought it was a confession, but when I went out to get it, it said my box no longer met government standards, and there would be no more deliveries until I got it fixed."

The hall erupted, and Gemery raised his voice. "Take it up with the feds," he said, just as someone in the front began waving both hands. Harry knew him, Caleb Barnes, a curmudgeon who owned an apple orchard on the main road, a mile or so above the dam.

"Speaking of things along the road," Barnes led in, "everybody knows I've had deer crossing signs in front of my property for years." Heads nodded. "Well, those deer have ruined my trees, and it's cost me plenty of money," he said, his voice rising. "I think I've done my duty, and I want the town to move the signs and let somebody else deal with the damned deer."

The whooping got louder, and as Gemery struggled for order, the fresh-out-of-jail poacher, Wilbur Findlay, leaped to his feet.

"I'll take 'em," he yelled.

Gemery waited for the hilarity to play out. "Oh, my," he said, "we've covered federal mailboxes and state deer crossing signs. Let's get down to the business of the town." The crowd quieted, but only because Woods then moved on to the matter of delinquent property taxes. Harry looked down at his copy of the *Annual Report* and thumbed through to the back to find the tax collector's report. It included two lists. The first cited one-year delinquents, and a shorter list had the names of those two years behind. Both lists included not only familiar deadbeats but also a smattering of those who had fallen on hard times. Henry McLaughlin fit both categories. Unless taxes on the two-year list were paid by July 1, Woods explained, the properties would be taken over and sold to the highest bidder. The amount poor Henry owed was $1,315, plus interest.

"Suitcase?" Diane whispered, pointing to Henry's name. Harry nodded, and Nibber mumbled that he'd get Debbie's vote when she came at noon, after the Sunrise closed.

The mention of Debbie made Harry grateful she hadn't been there for the tax report, as the discussion would only have stirred up her anxiety about paying her own taxes. Only last week she had told Harry and Nibber that she didn't know what she was going to do about next year's bill, and she was getting more and more tempted by Molony's offer to buy her out.

As if on cue, Nibber cocked his head toward the front row where Molony was in deep conversation with Spike Perkins, chairman of the Belfry Planning Committee.

"Bastard's scheming," Nibber muttered.

"No doubt about that," Harry replied. For the past few years, Molony had been throwing in low bids on tax-acquired property and making fat profits on the re-sales. At the moment, he was apparently cultivating his friendship with Perkins, who knew the comings and goings of local real estate better than anybody.

Woods moved to the end of her report, commenting on the capital fund account, being carried forward for what she called Belfry's "wish list." One wish was for the town to acquire shore property that could be used for public access to the water. The other was to solve the problem of cramped facilities at Town Hall.

The account, built from occasional budget surpluses, had grown to more than $250,000. Not enough, Woods said, to move ahead with either project. "And we won't be adding any money this year," she warned. "We're already over budget on snow plowing, and we can't borrow any more until we've paid off the debt on the new dam."

"Ouch!" Harry muttered. Mention of the new dam would raise the hackles of those who had opposed the project in the first place, and worse, sour the mood when he made his case for the spillway later on.

"We're dead," Nibber shrugged. "We'll probably get a public beach first, then wait until it washes out in a flood before we get money to fix the spillway."

Harry frowned. The wish list projects weren't just about money. The question of a town beach had been on the agenda since folks first realized that most of the good shore property on both Grand Pond and Finger Lake had been bought up, and the owners of the most tempting access places had built fences and put up 'no trespassing' signs. Even so, the Business Group kept pushing for the town to buy a beach and landing of its own, arguing that it was tough to promote Belfry as a tourist destination when tourists had no way to the water when they came. The state had boat marinas on both lakes, but they weren't picnic places and swimming wasn't allowed.

Nibber had made it plain he didn't give a damn about the tourists, but it wasn't right that local kids who lived back from the water had no place to swim. Harry fretted about the liability.

As for the town hall, most agreed something had to be done. Located near Belfry's lone blinker light at the intersection of the highway and the main road to Watford, the building was far too small. The food pantry had taken over the entire damp basement, and the main floor of the one-story building bulged with shared offices and file cabinets. Nibber thought they should find a bigger building, or build a new one. Harry thought an addition would be good enough.

"We can't do anything about either of these projects just now," Woods explained, "but we do need to be ready in case the right properties come up for sale before the next Town Meeting." Gemery followed with a call for the adoption of the next article in the warrant, authorizing the board to take money from the reserve account for any property that fit the approved plans. It passed, without objection.

It was already noon, and Gemery declared a recess for lunch, taking note that the Lions Club was selling soft drinks and hot dogs in the back kitchen. Some headed that way while others opened picnic baskets, and Harry was pleased when the general atmosphere improved with the mixed fragrances of tuna fish, hard-boiled eggs, and fried onions.

He and Nibber headed for the kitchen where Nibber ordered a hot dog and began to bathe it in catsup when

Gus Gammon whopped him on the back, sending a fresh red streak down the front of his newly washed Dam Committee T-shirt. "Thanks for saving Joyful Waters," Gammon exclaimed. "Let me know what you need from the mill."

"Thanks," Nibber said, wiping at his newest nib. "Hope to start next week if the weather holds fair."

Harry left them and elbowed his way through several Knight kids to get to the counter where he ran square into the Deacon and Molony. Harry could see that they were about to ignore him so he stood in their way. "Can we sign you boys up on the church renovation crew?" he said, forcing a pleasant smile.

"Well, of course," the Deacon replied between clenched teeth, "although my back's still sore."

"How else can we be sure it's done right?" Molony chirped as the pair moved back into the big hall.

Harry got his hot dog and moved to the condiment table where Mal Grandbush had managed to back Aidan Brown into a corner. The librarian was just then asking the trooper if Salome was getting pre-natal care while she was in jail, and Harry watched as Brown turned frantically and pretended to hail someone on the other side of the room so he could make his escape.

Debbie arrived just as Gemery called the afternoon session to order, and when Harry returned to his seat, Nibber was briefing her on the morning's proceedings. "Thanks Nibber," she cooed. "I feel like I haven't missed a thing." She lowered her voice. "And by all means, the suitcase for poor Henry."

It was time to deal with the several articles on town donations to social service agencies, and the first was for five hundred dollars for the Red Cross. The motion was defeated by a resounding voice vote. Diane made a note.

Next up was a request for two thousand to support the Belfry summer recreation program, and karaoke leader, Durwood Green, quickly objected. "Trouble with kids today is they can't think up a thing to do for themselves," he said. "We didn't have no summer rec program when we were kids, and we got along just fine."

"No, we didn't," Nibber muttered to Harry. "And we remember the summer day when we were kids when Durwood was playing with matches and burned down a boathouse over on Mosher stream." The motion failed. Diane made another note.

Although the afternoon session had begun, Henry McLaughlin was altogether sober when he led the fight for a thousand dollars to support the Cebennek Behavioral Health program, and voters also let in a hundred for Memorial Day flags along the road by the cemetery. An article appropriating two thousand for the town's Fourth of July celebration passed, but only after it was amended to exclude the purchase of fireworks. Diane made a third note.

The afternoon wore on, and by the time Gemery called on Malvine Grandbush for the library report, it was plain to see that folks had begun to lose interest. Mal, face flushed with excitement, bustled proudly to the front and began with a quote she was careful to say came from Samuel Johnson. "No place affords more striking conviction of the vanity of human hopes than a public library." She waited for the idea to sink in, but it didn't, and the assembly began to drift from their seats and chat with one another.

"The natives are restless," Harry said, noticing that Nibber looked a little green as he stared blankly at the murals across the way. "I'm gonna need riot gear by the time I get up there." Diane patted his hand.

At first unfazed by the wandering crowd, Mal plowed on with her prepared remarks, quoting Longfellow. "Oh," she said, spreading her arms to embrace the unfocused audience, "the love of learning, the sequestered nooks, and all the sweet serenity of books." She droned on to recite the year's count of library patrons, divided by sex and age.

Only when she had finished with the numbers did she realize that no one was paying attention at all, and her sweetness evaporated in an instant. She raised her voice. "Never mind the Goddamned vanity of human hopes and the sweet serenity of books," she screeched, "I need money, and I need it now." Heads snapped. Jaws dropped.

Harry turned to Nibber. "Bi-polar, you think?"

"Nah," Nibber answered. "Just a librarian."

With the audience now in rapt and fearful attention, Mal continued her case. The library had also outgrown its building, she said, and the Library Friends had begun to raise money for a new building. Harry looked at Diane, a devoted member of the group that not only enjoyed the books but also the wealth of gossip provided by the librarian.

"While we wait for a better day," Grandbush continued, "we have to have money to operate." She proceeded to remind voters of the "ghastly" cost of books, and the "pittance" of her own pay, and demanded that Gemery call for a vote. The yeas and nays were not clear, but after a hasty and fearful count of hands Gemery ruled that she had her money.

Harry straightened his only tie and strode fretfully to the front. The Dam Committee report was the last item of the day, and folks were already gathering their coats and picnic baskets. "First," he said, forcing a smile, "I want to thank you all for approving the money for a new dam. It's working just fine, but ..."

The "but" hung out a second, and then Harry bravely moved on. "But you all know the spillway is in bad shape, so bad in fact that we are not getting full advantage of the new dam because we have to hold back water to avoid wrecking the spillway. It's not good management."

"You're right about that," Molony shouted out. The Deacon stood and made one clap of his hands, looked around for support, didn't find any, and sat down.

A number of people had already begun to put on their coats when Harry continued. "The last article on today's agenda is to let the town raise fifty thousand dollars to repair the spillway, and I hope you will support it."

Gemery asked for discussion, and Danny Gould spoke up. Harry knew he would. "We didn't need a new dam and we don't need a new spillway," the former keeper said. "That spillway's been working fine for more than a hundred years, and besides, we ain't gonna have much rain this summer anyway."

Harry figured the old man had been reading pig spleens again, but he spoke up bravely. "We don't any of us know how much rain we're gonna get this summer," he said, "but the day is gonna come." He waited, shuffled his feet. Nobody raised a hand. Minds were made up. Some folks were already out the door.

Gemery called for a vote.

The "nays" were loud and overwhelming.

13

Diane padded into the kitchen and poured a cup of coffee. Harry and Winston were watching the morning news, and she patted them both on their heads. "Did you make the withdrawal?"

"I did. At six," Harry answered. "Winston stood guard while I went up over the garage. It's in the refrigerator."

"The refrigerator?"

"In a paper bag, next to the milk. Can't be too careful. You never know who might come tap, tap, tapping."

Diane retrieved the bag, went to the table and began to address one of several large, brown Manila envelopes she had spread out the night before. "Use your left hand," Harry said.

"I'm right-handed."

"Disguise your writing."

"Honestly, Harry, there's no way anybody's going to trace any of this back to us."

"And another thing," he said, continuing with his security measures, "I'm headed over to Joyful Waters to help Nibber this morning, but first I'll drive up the road to Nice and post the envelopes there. That way, there won't be any tie to Belfry, or to us."

"That would be nice." Diane played on the tired joke about the neighboring town, named by its first settler, a homesick Frenchman whose neighbors knew little about France and no French at all, and pronounced Nice with a long 'i.'

"Will you be putting any notes in there?" Harry asked warily, nodding at the envelopes.

"A couple of short ones," she said. "The Red Cross and Hospice don't need any, but there's a thousand bucks going to the Belfry Volunteer Fire Department, and we need to make sure they spend it on a resuscitator and not on one of those fancy toys they like to buy. And, oh yes, I'll put a note in the one with two thousand for the summer rec program, and send it to Susan Hanson. That's it."

"Keep 'em short and sweet," Harry warned. "And what about the Fourth of July fireworks?"

"Later. We'll put cash in the collection coffee can at Knight's Store. They'll be putting it out about the time the tourists arrive. Tourists love fireworks."

"There's always a few other collection cans there," Harry said. "Sometimes for worthy causes. We'll keep an eye. What about poor Henry?"

"We can take care of Henry on the way to the Sunrise tonight. Town Hall will be closed, and I'll sneak his tax payment in the letter slot."

It took her a half-hour to address all the envelopes, and Winston was already in the passenger seat when Harry got in the truck. He gave the dog a gentle shove so he could open the glove compartment and hide the envelopes, and Winston didn't like it. Harry wound down the window to cheer him up.

It was the last day of March, and when they passed by the entrance to the state boat landing, they could see fishermen lined up with their trucks, hauling shacks off the ice before the deadline. "Good riddance to the farters," Harry said.

Diane didn't like the name, but Harry told her it was a perfect fit for guys who spent all day in a small, overheated tin shack, drinking beer and eating propane fried sausage.

When they pulled onto the highway and passed Lake Lodge, Harry noticed the white pickup was nowhere in sight, but a green sedan with Vermont plates was parked out front. "The agent Donihue has rented himself another car," Harry muttered. "Here one day and gone the next, just like the Nurse. If I didn't know better, I'd say they're a tag-team."

Harry slowed at the dam, and looked out the window to check. The water level on Grand Pond was down several inches. He made a mental note to tell Nibber he could narrow up the gate. When they came up to the church, Nibber was already there, guiding one of Gus Gammon's trucks, loaded with foundation timbers and backing onto the lawn. Nibber spotted them and waved. He looked puzzled as they drove on by.

The road away from the lakes led up-hill through the woods, then flattened out into what was once broad pasture land, but now was slowly being eaten away by housing developments and sub-divisions, each with interrupting gates and fences. The welcoming sign at the town line read **THIS IS NICE**, and Harry observed to Winston that it wasn't really that nice anymore.

The town center at the intersection with Finger Lake Road was only a shadow of its lively past. The general store had been boarded up for ages, and weeds were growing through the crumbling cement sidewalks. Next door, meters on the pumps at the vacant Texaco station were rusted in at sixty-five cents a gallon. Across the road, Harry saw that the long building near the railroad tracks, once a feed and grain mill, had taken on yet another life as a combination tattoo parlor, thrift shop, and video store. The only building still in good shape was the tiny white post office next door. It wasn't yet open, and there were no cars in sight. Harry wheeled up to the blue collection box and stopped only long enough to push Winston back on the seat, pull out the envelopes, and shove them in the slot.

Harry glanced in the rear view mirror a dozen times on the way back to Belfry, and when they arrived at the church, Nibber came down the lawn to greet them. "Where you been?" he asked.

Harry looked around carefully before he answered. "Made a drop," he mumbled. Nibber caught on, changed the subject.

"Seen the paper?"

Harry shook his head. He hadn't.

"Salome's trial's set for April 21. Three weeks from now. You'll have to take the day off. Maybe two."

"For sure," Harry said. "Don't think you'll be covering this one by yourself."

Winston scampered off to greet the small crew of volunteers, several of them on their knees, struggling to place large jacks under the floor joists. Gammon directed the operation, barking orders. Neither the Deacon nor Molony were anywhere in sight, but Peppard was there, wielding a rake, huffing and puffing as he pulled debris from under the building. He spotted them and walked over, all smiles. "This is a day the Lord has made," he said, brushing at his broad front before reaching to scratch Winston's chin. "Joyful Waters will live again. In the meantime, you boys will want to know we've moved Sunday services across the road to the Grange for the duration."

"Thanks," Nibber said, "but we weren't planning ..." Harry cut him off with a glare, and Nibber changed the subject, pointing to the stretch of lawn out back where he had begun to frame up the new belfry. "Did that during the week, working by myself," he said. "Pretty good, I'd say, considering there weren't any plans. I'm going by an old photo Mal brought from the library."

"Working from a picture?" Harry was doubtful, and Nibber began to expand on the details when the roar of a chain saw cut him off. Old man Gammon was on the ground, slicing the rotten support timbers into manageable pieces, and waving instructions on the placement of the jacks. Harry and Nibber headed over to help just as Henry McLaughlin came up the front lawn, carrying a six-pack. "Brought lunch," he yelled, pointing at the beer.

Nibber started to shout, but when the chain saw suddenly went quiet, he spoke calmly. "Told you yesterday, Henry. No beer for lunch." Nibber made a face, and poor Henry sheepishly put the six-pack in the shade, under Peppard's movable letter sign.

"Forgot," he said meekly, heading off toward the others.

Harry looked at Nibber. "He's working for you?"

"Diane said I could hire him. Thought you wouldn't mind. We're not paying him much."

"It's not wise to give poor Henry any cash."

"I give him a few bucks for spending," Nibber said. "But the most of it goes into a savings account at The Old People's Bank. Connie Bonney set it up, a two-person book. We both have to sign."

"Perfect," Harry said before they joined the crew in the slow work of raising the jacks an inch at a time, around and around the building. Peppard wasn't doing any heavy lifting, but he kept things picked up, standing back every now and then to affirm that the slowly rising church was most certainly a sign from God.

The Deacon and Molony showed up at noon, just as the crew was ready to break for lunch. Nibber kept an eye on the six-pack and passed out sandwiches delivered by Kerri Woods, courtesy of the Crimson Crafters.

"We'd love to stay," the Deacon said, "but I've got some pieces in the spring gun show in Watford this afternoon, and we really oughta be there."

"Well, it sure is nice of you two to help out, Mr. Jalbert," Nibber said with a wry grin. "Maybe you wouldn't mind running up to Knight's to get us some soda?" The Deacon looked at Molony, who shrugged, and the two went off to the store.

By mid-afternoon, the church was blocked up all around, and the crumbling old timbers had been pulled out and stacked on the lawn. Peppard said he'd get a bonfire permit next week, and they'd have a hot dog and marshmallow fundraiser.

Nibber decided it was a good time to call it quits. "Gus will run lines during the week," he said to the crew, "and Henry and I will work on the belfry. Next Saturday, when you boys come back, we'll set the new timbers and let Joyful Waters back down."

* * * *

Harry and Nibber agreed to meet at the Sunrise in an hour. Winston, still in a snit over the shoving, chose to ride with Nibber, and Harry went to get Diane, who was surprised to see him home so early. "This will work out fine," she said excitedly. "Wash up and we'll make the drop at Town Hall on the way."

"How much did you put in for Henry?" Harry asked when they turned onto the highway for the short ride up to the blinker.

"The *Town Report* says he owes thirteen hundred-fifty," Diane said, "but I'm not sure exactly how to calculate the interest, and I couldn't very well ask. I added a hundred for good measure."

Harry drove around the back of Town Hall and turned off his headlights. "How the heck do you plan to see your way to the door without lights?" Diane groaned.

"Can't be too careful," Harry explained. "You flash 'em once when I get out of the truck, and I'll get the lay of the land." They waited until there was no traffic, and he ran to the door, stumbling once on the steps in the dark before he managed to cram the envelope in the letter slot. "There," he said after he groped his way back to the truck. "Now, poor Henry won't lose his house."

"This is getting to be a lot of fun," Diane observed as they drove on to the Sunrise, "and wait 'til you hear what else I've planned." Harry was curious, but didn't have a chance to follow up. Nibber was waiting, and he wrenched open Harry's door before they'd come to a full stop.

"Winston's in my truck," Nibber said, pointing. "The weather's mild, and he'd rather have a nap on the seat than wait at home."

"He's not going home with you, anyway," Harry said. "I'll get him when we leave, and I hope it's not late. I'm not in the mood for another whole night of karaoke."

* * * *

By the time they settled in to their usual booth, Darlene Ruff had finished with her warm-up, and the poacher, Wilbur Findlay, was at the microphone doing a lusty Leon Redbone imitation of *She Ain't Rose*.

She ain't Rose, but she ain't bad.
She ain't easy, but she can be had.

"I'd call that an unfortunate follow-up for Darlene," Diane observed as the good old boys at the bar slapped their knees and held onto their sides.

Something about the song reminded Harry of Salome, and he turned to Diane to ask if she'd heard the trial date was set. "Saw it in the paper," she said, "and I've been thinking. I don't know much about these things, but I do know that when you plead self-defense it's up to you to prove your case. No witnesses. No jury. She's going to have to take the stand and convince the judge, one on one."

"If she's as cool with him as she was with me, she'll have him in the palm of her hand," Nibber said. "Anyway, the truth will always set you free."

"Don't go biblical on me," Harry said. "Who knows what the truth is in this case, anyway?"

Henry McLaughlin had followed Wilbur, and Harry could tell poor Henry had found his six-pack from under Peppard's church lawn sign, because he was badly slurring the words to *I Drink Alone*, and Durwood Green was trying to coax him off the singing stool. "We'll take a short recess," Green said when he finally got hold of the microphone.

Molony and the Deacon walked in during the pause, and the Deacon waved cheerily from across the room. "Sorry we couldn't help out much today," he said. "Mr. Molony has to show some property next Saturday, but I'll be there if my Jeep starts."

"I'll pick you up," Harry yelled back. Nibber and Diane were more surprised than the Deacon. "I'm not letting him off," Harry said, "even if I have to drag him."

The evening fizzled out fast, and Emily Boulette came by to say it was the worst karaoke night in a long time. She blamed it on the good weather. Customers ate their meals and left. Molony and the Deacon were gone before nine. At 9:30, Emily said she was closing early, and Debbie stopped at the table to say they could all meet in a few minutes.

"That reminds me," Harry said. "What's this meeting about, anyway? You didn't call it, did you?" He looked at Nibber.

"Not me," Nibber said. "Diane did, although she's not a member."

"It's not an official Dam Committee meeting," Diane said. "Just an excuse to get together."

"I'm familiar with that approach," Harry said, looking at Nibber.

Debbie returned to the table, clutching something in her hand, a strange look on her face. "What?" Nibber asked as she slid into the booth next to him.

"You're not going to believe this," Debbie said, pausing to catch her breath. "First of all, when the Deacon and Molony cashed up, Molony put the heat on, said he wanted to get together so he could make another offer on my property. That didn't surprise me. He's always making new offers, but they never go up very much." She looked down at her hand. "But what surprised me was that when the Deacon paid his side of the tab, this is what he gave me." She spread a twenty-dollar bill on the table, and the others bent over for a close look. Harry figured it out first, and jumped back. Andrew Jackson had a perfect quarter-inch hole through his forehead. "I'll be damned," he said. "Peppard said there was 'almost' a thousand dollars in the envelope. The Deacon skimmed it."

"He's a thief," Nibber almost shouted, "and a bloomin' ignoranus."

"You mean ignora*mus*," Diane suggested.

"No," Nibber replied. "An ignoramus is a stupid person. Peppard is a stupid ass."

Harry placed a hand over the twenty as Emily came out of the kitchen to give her usual instructions. "Turn out the lights. Lock the door," she said. "Didn't know you guys were having a meeting tonight."

"Not an official meeting," Nibber answered. "Administrative details."

"And we don't even know what the administrative details are," Harry added.

"This is rather simple," Diane said when the place was quiet. "But first," she said, turning to Debbie, "I need to ask you some personal questions, if you don't mind."

"You know I don't mind," Debbie said, brushing her long hair away from her face and smiling at Nibber.

"How much is Molony offering you for your property?"

"He says he'll give me two hundred and fifty thousand."

"How much is it worth?"

"I had an appraiser come from Watford," Debbie said. "He says I should ask four hundred thousand and take three-fifty if I can get it."

Nibber looked mystified, but for Harry, the lights were beginning to come on. "Sounds about right to me," he said. "Ten acres, nice shore property on Finger Lake, a fine house and barn. I'd say at least three-fifty."

"Here's what I'm thinking," Diane said, slowly looking from face to face. "Belfry desperately needs a new town hall, with parking, and also some good shore property for public use. Susan Woods spelled it all out at Town Meeting." Diane waited. More lights came on. "Debbie's place is perfect for both of these things. The town already has two-fifty put aside. Debbie needs a hundred more."

"The suitcase!" Nibber's eyes lit up.

"Yup." Diane sat back, a satisfied look on her face, and Debbie stared straight ahead, unblinking. Harry put his hand on his chin, went over the idea in his head. The idea was altogether too simple. There had to be something wrong. Nibber spoke first. "They won't find a better piece of property for a town hall," he said. "The farmhouse is twice as big as what they have now, and it's in good shape. And there aren't any other sandy beaches on either lake that haven't been taken over and blocked off. Sounds like a two-for-one deal to me."

"And there's something else," Diane said. "It doesn't have to be part of the deal, but if the library took over the barn, it would be a charming place to re-locate. Plenty of parking, right there with the rest. If the town gave it to them, they could keep the money they've already raised, and use it to renovate."

"What will Debbie do with the hundred thousand cash?" Harry was still looking for the hitch.

"That's the beauty of it," Diane said. "She can live off it and bank the money she gets from the Sunrise."

"She could deposit it in the bank if she wanted to," Nibber offered. "A little bit at a time. Tell Connie Bonney it came from the sale of her folks' antiques."

Harry finally came around. "OK," he said, "so what's the next step?"

"I'd say Debbie pays a visit to Susan Woods and spells it out," Diane suggested.

"Fine with me," Harry said. "The town fathers have the authority to accept, voted at Town Meeting. They'll jump at it."

"Yes," Nibber said with a grin. "And won't it be grand to see Bolony's face when he gets the word?"

14

Something had the crew at the Gammon Mill in turmoil, and workers flitted around the big saw, lifting their ear protectors and yelling back and forth above the screaming blade. Harry lunged at the red alarm button. When the whirring stopped, he discovered the culprit was the day's edition of the *Watford Journal*. "Gimme that damn paper," he yelled, "and for gawdsakes pay attention to what you're doing."

One of the men stepped forward and sheepishly handed him the offending newspaper, pointing to a smudged item where it was folded. "Look here," he said. "See for yourself. Belfry's got her own Easter Bunny."

Harry waited until everything was back in order before he looked down to see what caused the stir. The headline on page six was tiny:

Mystery Donor Saves
Summer Rec Program

Beneath, a short article quoted Susan Woods as saying that, only days after the Town Meeting had rejected a request to fund the Belfry summer recreation program, somebody had made an anonymous gift of two thousand dollars to keep it going. The town manager called the gift "a miracle," and "a blessing for our youth"

and made a special appeal to the donor to come forward
and be properly thanked.

Harry watched the crew take another slice off a pine
log and chock it up to dry. He thought for sure they had
taken every precaution to hide the suitcase and disguise
the drops, but they hadn't counted on the publicity. Bad
enough that Peppard had announced the donation to
Joyful Waters from the pulpit, but now the town
manager had told the newspaper about the anonymous
gift to Belfry. It was only Friday. By the end of the
weekend, everybody in town would be making wild
guesses about who had the money and where it came
from. And, little doubt, Mal Grandbush would be leading
the gossip parade with some whacko theory that was just
as likely to land on the Dam Committee as anyone else.
His heart thumped. They were in trouble, for sure. It was
only a matter of time before the feds came to make an
arrest, or worse, the Nurse stormed the garage with an
Uzi.

Harry felt the sudden urge to talk with Nibber, whose
quirky assessments of life's troubles were somehow
always calming. Diane wouldn't be any help. Instead,
she'd be in a renewed state of anxiety over harboring the
suitcase, and Debbie wouldn't know what to make of any
of it. He checked his watch. Two hours until noon, and
he'd be off for a long weekend. First, he'd run up and see
Nibber, and at two, go with Debbie for her proposition
meeting with Susan Woods. On Monday, he was going to
Watford, to at least catch the first day of Salome's trial.
He'd felt a little guilty about asking for so much time off,

but he was grateful that Gus Gammon approved. Harry had explained to the old man that he needed Friday afternoon to help Debbie with what he called "tax worries," and he left it at that. Gus had readily agreed, didn't ask questions, but when Harry said he wanted to take Monday off as well, the old man hesitated before he finally agreed Harry could go because of his "special ties" to Salome. Now, Harry grew uneasy about having anyone think he had any special ties to the O'Neil affair, and he fretted away the rest of the morning, punching off the clock at the very stroke of noon.

* * * *

When he roared up the rutted driveway, Harry was relieved to find his friend at home. "Can't stay," Harry said, sticking his head through the open cabin door. "Seen the paper?"

Nibber was seated at the kitchen table, and Harry quickly noticed the customary disarray had been somehow rearranged. Dirty dishes had been moved from the table to the sideboard, and the only floor lamp, its shade askew, was out of the corner by the television and placed near Nibber's chair.

"Yup," Nibber answered without looking up. "Saw the paper. You seen the fire station?"

"Haven't been down that way today."

"Big bed sheet over the truck bay." Nibber said. "It's a sign thanking whoever gave money for the new resuscitator. I think they spelled it wrong. We'll ask Diane."

"Sweet Jesus!" Harry slouched in the empty chair at the table. "We never figured on getting this kind of attention."

"I know." Nibber made a wry smile. "It's a damn shame. You can't hardly give anything away these days without somebody up and thanking you."

It was the response Harry expected, and he paused as he gazed around the cluttered room where everything seemed out of place except for Nibber's prized collection of *Playboy* magazines, still evenly lined on one long shelf along the back wall. "We're gonna get caught," Harry persisted.

"Never." Nibber didn't look up as he poked away on his hand calculator.

"What on earth are you doing?" Harry asked.

"Taxes."

"What's the rush? There's still a few days left."

"Ice will be going out soon," Nibber said, "and I'll have docks to put in. Saw Colt's Feet bloomin' back of the cabin yesterday. Be cutting grass before you know it. Meantime, I'm working at the O'Neils', replacing the sheetrock Doc ruined, and then we've got that big project at Joyful Waters. On top of all that, there's the dam to watch."

"Dam's doin' fine," Harry observed. "We still might get a big rain, but unless we do, we just might get out of the run-off without any trouble at all." Nibber nodded and went back to work.

"Short form or long form?" Harry was curious.

"I could use the short form, but the long one makes for a better record."

"Record of what? You only take cash. I'm surprised you pay taxes at all."

Nibber looked hurt. "Everybody is supposed to pay taxes," he said. "Just that I do it a little different, that's all."

"Different?"

"First, I figure out how much taxes I want to pay, and then I adjust my income to make it come out right."

"Most people do it the other way around."

"Most people are too lazy to figure it out." Nibber put down the calculator and went on to explain that he paid quarterly and made sure he always got a refund. "Wait 'til next year," he said.

"Next year?"

"Think about the deduction I'm gonna have when I put in for the work at Joyful Waters."

"For Pete's sake, Nibber, anybody who has charitable deductions greater than their income is certain to be investigated."

"We'll worry about that next year," Nibber replied. "In the meantime, we won't worry about anything at all. All the fuss about charitable giving around here will eventually blow over, just like most everything else."

"It'll blow *up* first." Harry looked at his watch. "Time to go. You comin'?"

"Nope," Nibber said. "Debbie and I talked about it. Woods might get the wrong idea if I went."

"Why won't she get the wrong idea if *I* go?"

"You're the father figure."

"Thanks." Harry said, moving toward the door. "Then I'll go get my daughter. She'll be waiting."

* * * *

As he had expected, Harry was in a better mood when he climbed back into the truck, and it lasted until he reached Town Hall, where Debbie was waiting on the same steps he had tripped on in the dark when he paid poor Henry's taxes. He could tell in a minute that she was jittery, and he began to wonder if she might accidentally spill the beans.

"Now don't you go getting nervous," Harry said when he greeted her. "Just be careful what you say, and this will all go just fine."

"Hope so," she said, wringing her hands, "but Nibber says Susan can sometimes be a ditz."

"Well, I suppose he would know about such things," Harry said, "but still, I'm pretty sure Susan will think you have a grand idea." He put his arm around Debbie's shoulder as the secretary ushered them into Susan's tiny office.

"Sorry for the mess," Susan apologized, moving stacks of papers off two folding chairs that barely fit in front of her cluttered desk. "The place has been in a zoo since Town Meeting, even more since Santa Claus came to town."

"Santa Claus?" Debbie didn't get it. "It's April."

"You know," Woods explained, "the anonymous gifts. We got two thousand dollars in tens and twenties for the summer rec program, and the fire department got its resuscitator. I heard the Red Cross got some, too. Sure would like to know who's doing this."

"So would I," Debbie went along. "Any ideas?"

"If it was summer, there'd be a few suspects among the rich people," Woods offered, "but I can't think of any locals who could do this, or even would if they could. If you want to know what I think, I think it all has to do with the O'Neil murder and the money Doc was hiding."

Harry uncrossed one knee and crossed the other, tried to be casual. "Who says he was hiding any money?"

"Everybody knows. Didn't you?"

Harry smiled weakly. "Well, it can't be Doc or Salome," he said. "He's dead and she's in jail."

"Well then, it's someone else."

Harry was set to probe further when Debbie cut in with a loud, deep breath. "I've come to make a proposal to the town," she began, folding her hands on her lap. "And it has to do with our Belfry wish list." She waited for Susan to catch up, then went on. "I was at Town Meeting," she said, "and I know we're looking for property for a bigger town hall and a public beach. My place could suit both purposes, and I'd like to offer it for the amount already put aside for these things."

Woods gazed out the window. Harry wondered why she did not seem more surprised. "Funny you should say that," she said, turning back. "Maybe I shouldn't be telling you this, but Jeff Molony was hanging around here yesterday, shootin' the breeze with me while he examined the list of tax acquired property."

"I'll bet," Harry inserted.

Woods was sidetracked. "Makes me think," she said. "I'm so glad poor Henry McLaughlin isn't on that list anymore. Speaking of miracles, I can tell you he paid his taxes at the very last minute."

Debbie and Harry swapped glances. "Oh, I'm so glad for him," Debbie gushed.

"Anyway," Woods went on, looking at Debbie, "Molony mentioned he was trying to buy your folks' place. He said he'd offered you two-fifty and that if you sold it to him, he would rent it a year or so until the town could raise enough more money to buy it."

"I'll bet," Harry repeated.

Woods ignored him. "Your place is perfect," she said to Debbie, "but there's something I don't understand." She flipped through a large ledger on the table beside her desk, and when she found what she was looking for, put her finger on the page. "Your place is worth more than the town can afford to pay, a hundred thousand more if you went by the tax appraisal. And, as you know," she added, "these appraisals are almost always below real value."

Debbie nodded. "I know all that," she said, "and I've given it a lot of thought." She looked down, and then lifted her head. "You see, my folks loved this town, and so do I. When they died, I thought I might go back to Connecticut to pick up where I left off, but I've come to realize how much I love Belfry, and I want to stay." She looked at Harry, who knew the main attraction wasn't Belfry.

"Money isn't everything," Debbie went on. "If the town gave me two-fifty for the property, that much besides the money I make at the Sunrise would give me enough to be comfortable in a more modest place. Sure, I could maybe make more money if I held on, but I'd like to think of the difference as a kind of memorial to my folks."

Harry wondered if she was laying it on a bit thick, but it didn't matter. Woods was buying. "I'd guess Molony won't be very pleased if you end up selling the place to the town for the same price he's offered," she said.

"You can bet on that." Harry was beginning to sound like a gambling parrot. Debbie said nothing, waited.

"I think you've made a splendid offer," Woods said finally. "Two of the town's biggest needs met with one piece of property. Lots of land, and it can all be saved. No need to chop it up and fence it off for some development. Perfect all around." Harry could tell she was counting up the plusses. "And, as you know," she went on, "Town Meeting gave the Board of Selectpersons the authority to make a land purchase if the right place came up before next year. I'm pretty sure they'll jump at this, but of course I have to take this kind of thing to them for approval."

"Not a problem," Debbie said. "I'm in no rush."

"By the way," Harry said, making his first real contribution, "the old barn is in perfect shape. It might make a great place for a bigger library."

"Funny you should say that," Susan said. "Molony mentioned that same idea yesterday." Harry held back on another sure bet. "I'll have a chat with Mal Grandbush," Susan said, "but I'll have to wait on that, else it will be in the newspaper before I get a chance to tell the board."

"You could bet on that." Harry couldn't help himself.

15

There had been an on-shore breeze all night, and in the morning Harry and Winston sat on the shore in the warm sun, listening to the tinkling of the ice as it broke into a million tiny crystals and slowly sank to the bottom of the pond. April 8 was early for ice-out, and while Harry had predicted it, a part of him wished it had held on a little longer to slow the run-off, put pressure on the spillway, and teach the dam repair nay-sayers a lesson.

"Dodged a bullet," Harry observed to Winston, who heard the sermon coming and ran off to do a celebratory dance through white mounds of mushy ice along the water's edge. Probably just as well, Harry thought to himself. Between the murder and the money, the village had enough to fuss about without having to deal with a springtime flood. The loons, he knew, would somehow know the ice was out, and they'd be back by nightfall to wail greetings to the new season and maybe bring back a sense of normalcy.

Winston returned and shook cold water on both Harry's thoughts and his trousers just as Diane shouted down from the house. "We'd better get a move on if we intend to get a seat at the courthouse. There's likely to be a big crowd."

Harry trudged up the bank and Winston followed, stopping once or twice to glance back longingly at the open and inviting lake.

"Oh, my," Harry said as he and Winston shook off in the entry, "what does one wear to a murder trial?"

"Something dark, I'd guess," Diane said as Harry ran upstairs to change. He returned in a minute, wearing jeans and a Navy blue sweater, slicking his hair with a wet hand. Winston groaned a pitiful good-bye as they went out the door.

* * * *

The downtown Watford streets were jammed, and a sizable crowd was converging on the old courthouse. A burly officer stood at the top of the granite steps, directing the mob of spectators and warning everybody, including folks without cameras, that pictures were not allowed.

Harry and Diane moved to a bench in the back where Nibber and Debbie held two places. Although he was dressed smartly in his official Dam Committee T-shirt, Nibber seemed uneasy. "Sure hope Salome doesn't see us," he said, wagging his head. "This makes me feel like a voyager."

"That would be a *voyeur*," Diane said.

"Yes," he replied. "Creepy."

"She won't see us in this mob," Harry said as he surveyed the crowded room. Even the un-needed jury box was filled with gawkers, including Mal Grandbush, who sat pertly in the front row, wearing a large flowered hat that blocked the view of Henry McLaughlin. Poor Henry was just then leaning around the brim to whisper into Mal's eager ear, and the sight gave Harry a sinking feeling. The news that he and Nibber had been on the ridge the night of the murder had no doubt already filtered from Deputy Kelly to Aidan Brown and on to poor Henry, who at that very moment was probably sharing the tidbit with Belfry's chief busybody.

Elsewhere, the room was peppered with familiar faces. The Gammons, Knights, Kerri Woods, and Emily Boulette were there, as was Hummer Humbolt, who must have sorted the mail early and closed the service window so he could join the mass exodus from Belfry.

Hummer sat up front in a clot of neighbors, including the Deacon and Molony. "Reminds me," Nibber said, pointing at Harry, "I want to thank you for bringing the Deacon to Joyful Waters on Saturday. He didn't do very much work, claimed he had a sore shoulder, but he helped a little, and we managed to get a lot done."

Harry allowed a tiny smile. "It was worth it to make the long trip down East Road to get him," he said. "I found out he wasn't lying when he said his Jeep was out of commission. Saw it up on jacks in the garage. Bolony might have brought him up to Joyful Waters, but he was off on some real estate deal. I'd never been to the Deacon's house before, and never met his wife. He keeps her under wraps. She's real tiny, like a mouse. Barely said a word. Just nodded to me when she answered the door, then scurried off to find him."

"What's the house like?" Diane wanted to know.

"Lots of Jesus pictures," Harry said, "and the man has a big collection of guns, all in cases around the walls. He said he had some of them in a gun show in Watford last year. Made me take a copy of the catalogue, as if I cared."

"Maybe he's getting up an army for the Lord," Nibber quipped just as a court officer ushered Salome and her lawyer Pasquale into the courtroom, and the place fell silent. Everybody leaned at once to have a look. Salome wore a plain blue frock dress, buttoned to the very top. Her blond hair was pulled back and tied in a ribbon that matched her dress, and when she sat down, she dabbed her eyes with a small, lacy handkerchief.

"Doesn't seem much like a murderer to me," Harry whispered to Diane. "Looks more like the mother in *Little Home on the Prairie*."

"Shush!"

"All rise!" The hefty officer spoke sharply, his thick neck threatening his collar button, and there was a general shuffling of feet as everybody stood and gaped as Judge Joe Parden walked slowly to the bench. Harry had imagined a scowling, stern-faced man, but instead Parden seemed like a grandfather from central casting – round, kindly face with pink cheeks, white hair, and blue eyes twinkling through gold-rimmed glasses.

The clerk called the case, and Parden promptly invited the prosecutor, Webster Dean, to make his opening statement. The *Watford Journal* had described the young state attorney as "tough and ambitious" and "eager for his first major trial," but as he walked stiffly to the bench, he looked like a pimply-faced high school kid, nervous and unsure of himself.

"Your honor," Dean squeaked, "we already know Salome O'Neil killed her husband Gregory O'Neil on the night of March 7 at the couple's home in Belfry. Of that, there can be no dispute. We have the murder weapon, and we will have the testimony of reliable witnesses that she has voluntarily and repeatedly confessed to killing her husband. The only unanswered question in this case goes to the matter of motive. The defense will say she shot him in self-defense. The state will show her actions were not taken to save her own life – not at all – but instead, that she killed her poor husband in cold blood within minutes after he peaceably returned to his home after three years of repaying his debt to society for a crime far less serious than murder."

Gaining steam and confidence, Dean turned and walked toward Salome. "This woman was not driven by fear at all," he said, pointing a bony finger. "Oh, no, we can't be fooled. This woman was driven by the most common motive for murder in the world – greed. Pure and simple greed." He paused and turned back to the bench. "We will show beyond a reasonable doubt that this woman killed her husband for his money." Dean was finished, and he seemed quite pleased with himself.

Harry glanced along the bench at the others, made a sour face. There it was again. The subject of Doc O'Neil's money was out in the air, this time in the glare of a well-publicized murder trial.

Diane was more worried about Salome. "I think she's in trouble," she said softly.

"It ain't over 'til the fat lawyer sings," Nibber quipped as the seasoned attorney strode to the bench.

"Mornin', judge," Pasquale had a big grin.

"Continue." Parden seemed not to like the familiarity, but Pasquale was undaunted, and he turned briefly to nod greetings in the direction of the juryless jury box, prompting Mal Grandbush to sit up quickly and return a tiny, gloved wave.

"Your honor," Pasquale boomed out, "the defense will of course stipulate that Salome O'Neil shot and killed her husband, and I'm grateful to my honored colleague for making reference to Doc O'Neil's return to society, as this will open the door to a discussion of the man's checkered past. It is important to my case."

Dean gave a hesitating shrug, and Pasquale continued. "There will be claims of a pile of money somewhere, and suggestions that this money is evidence of my client's guilt," he went on. "The curious thing, judge, is that no one has produced a single nickel of that money. Mrs. O'Neil doesn't have it. The state doesn't have it. Even the feds, who would no doubt claim it if there was any, don't have it. This is all fine with us, your honor, because unless somebody can produce the money, how on earth will the state be able to prove she killed him for it?"

Pasquale was on a roll. "No, your honor, my client didn't shoot her husband for his money. In fact, the truth is quite the opposite, and she is ready to explain it all.

When she has told her story, I feel quite certain you will reasonably and comfortably conclude that she shot Doc O'Neil to save her own life."

Pasquale beamed at the judge for a few seconds before he headed back to his seat, stopping briefly in front of the prosecutor's table and pointing his finger at Dean. "Show me the money!" he boomed. The gallery erupted in giggles. Parden glared, rapped his gavel, and waited for quiet before he instructed Dean to begin his case.

The first witness was Kelly Hallowell, who stood proudly in her starched sheriff's uniform to take the oath, her polished, brown leather holster flaring precariously close to the judge's head. Nibber noticed, and began to snicker. Diane jabbed him with her elbow.

Dean asked Hallowell for a report on the critical times on the night of the murder, and she had barely begun to answer when the judge broke in. "Eastern times, if you please."

Kelly flushed, apologized, and explained that she had been called at 5:10 p.m. and arrived at the O'Neil house ten minutes later. Dean inquired who was in the house when she arrived, and Hallowell said Fred Jalbert met her at the door. "Everybody calls him 'the Deacon,'" she said. "He's from Joyful Waters. Said Mrs. O'Neil had called him, and explained he'd arrived only a minute or two before. Otherwise," she said, "the only other people around were Mrs. O'Neil and the deceased."

Dean invited her to describe the scene, and Kelly said the victim was slumped forward, facing upstairs, at the turn on the landing. "He was quite a mess," she said, wrinkling her face. "I knew right away he was dead, but I checked his pulse anyway. He was quite dead."

Asked to describe Salome's behavior, Kelly said she was "a wreck," and that "she kept repeating that her husband had come after her with a knife and that she had no choice but to shoot him." Pasquale flashed a smug smile and said he had no questions.

Next up was Trooper Brown, who said he had arrived five minutes after Hallowell. "I went by the book," he said, "bagged the weapon, ordered the place ribboned off, and radioed for a detective and a state prosecutor." He paused. "And a hearse." Again, Pasquale wasn't interested in cross-examining.

Dean returned to his table and brought two plastic bags to the bench. "I would like to introduce as Exhibit A the weapon used to kill Mr. O'Neil, a .357 model Ruger." He handed the judge one of the bags. "At the same time, I'd like to introduce Exhibit B, the weapon – if you can call it that – that Mrs. O'Neil claims her husband used to threaten her."

"Objection!" Pasquale rose to his feet. "I don't mind having the second weapon introduced," he said, "but I do object to Mr. Dean's characterization of it."

"Sustained." Parden didn't like it either.

"I withdraw the comment," Dean said, "and next I'd like to call Mr. Scott Paradis, the state forensic expert who was called to the scene that night and subsequently examined both of these weapons." Paradis took the stand, and began by saying he had extracted the slug from a two-by-four behind the sheetrock wall on the landing, and that he later established that ballistic tests had proven that the Ruger was indeed the murder weapon. Dean then asked if Paradis had determined the owner of the gun.

"Mrs. O'Neil said it belonged to her," Paradis said, "but it was not possible to prove it."

"Why not?" Dean asked.

"Because we have only her word," he said. "The serial number has been removed." He took the weapon and pointed under the pistol grip. "Here," he said, "near the lanyard loop. You can see the numbers have been filed off."

"So, it's an illegal weapon?" Dean inquired.

"Not really," Paradis said. "Maine doesn't require handgun registration. Sellers have to register serial numbers, but this gun was not sold. The defendant would have needed a permit to conceal and carry the weapon, but so far as we know, it never left the house."

Dean was unfazed. "Okay," he said, "so maybe there's nothing illegal here, but would you agree that a weapon with its serial numbers removed raises suspicions that it might have been acquired for the purpose of committing a crime?"

"Objection," Pasquale bellowed. "Calls for speculation on the part of the witness."

"Sustained."

"Did you examine the gun for fingerprints?" Dean asked.

"I did."

"Whose prints did you find?"

"Mrs. O'Neil's." He pointed to the wooden grip. "A thumb print here, just above the big scratch." He pointed to the place on the weapon, and held it up. Even in the back row, Harry could see the scar on the grip.

"Any others?" Dean asked.

"No."

Dean moved on, fished the knife out of the second bag and used two fingers to dangle it in front of the judge before he turned to Paradis. "Do you recognize this thing?"

"I took it from the victim's hand that night."

"How would you describe it?"

"Table flatware."

"In your experience, is table flatware ordinarily used to kill someone?"

"Objection!" Pasquale bellowed from his seat.

"Sustained."

Dean was finished, and Pasquale finally had a question. He took the kitchen knife and held it in front of Paradis. "Never mind whether this is an *ordinary* weapon," he said, "would you agree that it could be used to kill?"

"Any blade can kill," Paradis replied.

"Thank you."

Dean announced the state was resting its case, and Judge Parden looked at his watch before declaring a recess until after lunch. "We will resume with the defense at one p.m.," he announced before gathering up his robe and disappearing behind the bench.

* * * *

The courtroom emptied quickly. Most of the crowd headed across the street to the Jurybox, a tiny lunch diner where lawyers, judges and clerks regularly mingled with defendants, accusers and hangers-on to get a quick meal between sessions. Harry knew the diner conversation would most likely be about the missing money, and didn't want to hear it. Instead, he suggested they skip into the nearby variety store and buy sodas and ready-made ham and cheese sandwiches. Nibber turned up his nose, said he and Debbie wanted to take a walk along the Cebennek.

When Harry returned with lunch, he and Diane sat down to eat on the sun-warmed granite steps. "Amazing," he said.

"What's amazing?"

"Nibber having a date without a chaperone."

"I'm proud of him," she laughed.

"I'll tell you something that's *not* good," Harry said, looking around to make sure they were alone. "All this talk about the money, that's what. It can't lead to anything but trouble."

Diane took a bite of her sandwich and hunched her shoulders. "In for a penny, in for a pound," she said. "Besides, we can't stop now. We've been very careful, and remember, we've already been able to spend nearly half the money without getting caught, or even having a finger pointed at us. From here on, we'll just have to be even *more* careful, that's all." She put an arm around his back. "You always worry for nothing," she said. "Don't things usually work out for you and me?"

Harry gazed across the street where knots of people were hanging around outside the diner. "Usually," he said, turning to gaze into her face. "But not always."

She took his hand. "It's all right," she said, her eyes growing misty. "Who knows? Maybe one of these days we'll turn that little office of yours back into a nursery."

The two ate in silence, watching the diner, when suddenly Mal Grandbush came out the door, spotted them, and fluttered across the street and up the granite steps. "Just the people I wanted to see," she said, sitting down between them, adjusting her big hat. "Actually, I was looking for Debbie. She can't be far."

"She and Nibber went for a walk," Diane said, "down by the river."

"Well, what do you know?" Mal's eyes grew big.

"I said, a *walk*," Harry was curt.

"I just wanted to thank her." Mal kept a steady course.

"For what?" Harry asked.

"Susan Woods told me about her generous contribution to the town. I'm sure you two know all about that, and about the possibilities for the library. It's wonderful. I'm so excited. Susan told me the selectpersons already know, but I can't tell a soul until they vote. Mum's the word. You know me."

"I do indeed." Harry shook his head.

Mal ignored him. "And what's your take on all this talk about this money they can't find?"

Harry rolled his eyes skyward where a pair of gulls was circling, their beady eyes fixed on his ham and cheese. He didn't answer. Diane pretended not to hear.

"There's plenty of theories," Mal said with a hint of invitation in her voice, "but I think I know who has the money."

At that moment, Harry took a chomp on his sandwich and accidentally nipped his finger. He yelped, and Mal jumped back. "Want to know who?" She asked, without skipping a beat.

"Who?" Harry gushed out the word and sent a tiny piece of crust wafting into Mal's big hat.

"Aidan Brown." The name hung in the air for a second, then she went on. "Think about it. He was there that night, right behind Kelly Hallowell. He was in charge. Had access to the whole place. I figure there was a bag of money around there somewhere, and he grabbed it. Makes sense to me."

Harry thought for a second he might let her story stand. She was no doubt still sore about Aidan's rebuff when she'd asked him about the murder that first night at the Sunrise, and the longer suspicions were focused on someone else, the better off they were. Mal Grandbush was, after all, a powerful force in directing local rumors. But, then he thought about the hapless trooper, and couldn't hold back.

"For God's sake, Mal, Aidan Brown is one of the most honest men we know, and he would never take money that didn't belong to him. Besides ..." He stopped mid-sentence, and a troubled look came over his face as he considered what he'd just said about himself.

16

The lunch crowd began to drift across the street from the Jurybox Diner, and Diane headed into the courtroom to reclaim their morning seats. Harry waited outside for Nibber and Debbie, who came from around the back of the building at the very last minute, holding hands and laughing. When they reached the top of the steps, Debbie flashed a quick smile, gave Harry a fast peck on the cheek, and went inside to find Diane.

"Hold on." Harry grabbed Nibber by the arm. "Had lunch?"

"Plain forgot."

"You're not well," Harry suggested. "*You* forgot to have lunch?"

Nibber nodded and pointed to the spotless front of his Dam Committee T-shirt as proof, then gestured over his shoulder with his thumb. "Don't look now," he said in a low voice, "but look at that."

"Impossible," Harry replied, looking back anyway. A man in a tan overcoat, head down, was coming slowly up the steps. Harry didn't recognize him until the man looked up, saw Harry, and quickly tugged down on the brim of his hat.

"Cripes," Harry gasped. "It's the freakin' Nurse!"

"Hurry up!" Nibber already knew. "We don't want to meet *that guy* again," he said as they knocked into each other as they both tried to get through the courthouse door at once.

"From the looks, I'd say he didn't want to meet us, either," Harry said when they were inside. He looked back to see the deputy point the Nurse to a single seat at the end of the last row, and he and Nibber sat down just as Judge Parden appeared at the bench, rapped his gavel, and cast a silent spell over the room. "I presume the defense is ready," the judge intoned, beckoning Pasquale with his finger.

"We are." Pasquale emphasized as he walked confidently to the bench, hands in his pockets, belly bulging over his belt. "Your honor," he began with a smile, "as I said this morning, the defense is willing to stipulate that my client, Salome O'Neil, shot her husband on the night of March 7. We further stipulate that she used the weapon introduced to the court as Exhibit A."

He paused a second or two before going on. "However, we do not agree Mrs. O'Neil is guilty of murder as charged, but instead we claim the unfortunate killing was in self-defense and entirely justified." He pulled his hands from his pockets and leaned close to the bench, causing the judge to recoil an inch or two. "Your honor," Pasquale said gravely, "I'm afraid the only witness to this sad incident is the defendant herself, and I call her at this time."

Every head tracked Salome as she made her way to the witness stand. She whispered a soft 'I do' to the oath and then sat down, smoothed her dress across her lap, and made a brief, furtive glance around the room before she turned and stared intently at Pasquale.

Harry watched her every move, then glanced around the room. Diane, Nibber and Debbie were hunched forward in their seats, mouths and eyes wide open. Mal Grandbush was crouched intently over the front rail of the jury box, and behind her, poor Henry half stood to peek through her flowered hat. In front, the Deacon loomed above the rest and, like a choir director, slowly pumped his hands, palms down, sending calming signals to his parishioner on the stand. Up back, the Nurse bent forward, head in his hands, his cap half covering his face.

"Mrs. O'Neil," Pasquale began. "I am well aware of your bereavement and of your suffering at the hands of your accusers." He shook his head sorrowfully. "However," he went on, "I'm sure you understand we have no choice but to ask you to testify on your own behalf so this court will know the real truth of this entire unfortunate matter."

She gave a tiny nod, and Pasquale continued. "This morning, my worthy colleague, Mr. Dean, mentioned that your husband, Gregory O'Neil, had just returned home after paying his debt to society," Pasquale glanced over at Dean, who winced. "Perhaps we can begin right there. Tell us, if you please, exactly why your husband happened to find himself in debt to society."

Salome seemed rehearsed, and she replied matter-of-factly. "He served a three year sentence in Ray Brook Prison on federal charges of dealing in illegal drugs."

"Would you say he was a mobster?"

"Objection!" Dean yelped.

"Overruled." Parden didn't hesitate.

"Yes."

"Did you visit him while he was in jail?"

"Yes."

"How many times?"

"Three."

"Only three visits in three years?"

"Yes."

"Why only three times?"

Salome took a deep breath. "Well, you see, the first time I went to see him was the week after he went to jail. I thought he'd be glad to see me, but right off he told me he had hidden a suitcase filled with money, a half-million or more." Harry blanched. Salome went on. "He said he would tell me where it was if I promised to go and get it and keep it for him until he got out of jail. He said I could use some of it if I had to."

Harry scanned his eyes along the bench and saw three monkeys, each one slouched with elbows on their knees. Diane's head was cupped in her hands, a finger in each ear. Nibber peeked through spread fingers, and Debbie held her hand over her mouth, an astonished look in her eyes.

Pasquale moved closer to Salome. "Did you agree to go and get the suitcase?"

"I did not."

"Why not?"

"I told him it was dirty money, and besides, I was afraid to have it. I said there were people willing to kill for it, and the feds were probably out looking for it as well. I told him I wanted nothing to do with it. I didn't even want to know where it was."

"And, what did your husband say to that?"

"He got very angry and threatened me. He said if I didn't get the money for him, I'd be sorry. He got himself into a terrible rage. I remember being glad there were bars between us."

"Was that the end of it?"

"No. I went back twice more, each time hoping he'd forget about it, but both times we fought about the money. The last time I went, I told him that if he didn't let go, I wouldn't come back to visit. He said he didn't care."

"And you never went back?"

"I never saw him again until the night he came home."

Pasquale went back to his table, picked up an envelope, and handed it to the judge. "This, your honor, is an affidavit from Ray Brook Prison, certifying that Mrs. O'Neil visited her husband only three times, all within the first month of his incarceration." Parden opened the letter, read it, passed it to Dean, then had it marked 'Exhibit C.'

"Do you have any idea where that suitcase of money is right now?" Pasquale asked.

"I don't."

"Did your husband mention it when he came home the night of March 7?"

"Oh yes. It came up right away, but he never said where it was."

Pasquale paused, paced purposefully back and forth in front of the bench, and returned to the stand. "Now," he said, looking pained, "I know this is going to be hard, but I'd like for you to describe to us exactly what happened that night. It's very important. Don't leave anything out. Take as much time as you need."

Salome adjusted herself in her seat and began. "I didn't know exactly when he was coming home," she said. "He'd called me in the middle of the week from Ray Brook. Told me he was coming home on Saturday, but he came a day early. Just before five o'clock."

"Where were you when he got there?" Pasquale interrupted.

"I was upstairs, in the bedroom, straightening things up. I heard the front door open, and I went to the top of the stairs and called down. He answered."

"What did he say?"

"He started right in. It was like he'd stayed mad for three years," Salome said, dabbing her cheeks with the handkerchief. "He started screaming that I'd betrayed him, and he called me terrible names."

"What names?" Pasquale interrupted.

"He said I was filthy trash." She put her head down. "And a disloyal bitch. He said over and over I was going to pay for not helping him."

"Go on."

"He went into the kitchen. I could hear him rummaging through the drawers, banging and yelling. I was terrified, and I went to the bedside stand and got the gun out of the drawer."

Her voice choked, and she lowered her head and continued wiping her eyes. When she looked up, black streaks of mascara were running down her cheeks. "After I got the gun, I went to the top of the stairs and saw him start up. He had a knife in his right hand, holding it way over his head, like this." She demonstrated. "He screamed he was going to kill me, and when he got to the landing where the stairs turn, I told him to stop and drop the knife or I'd shoot him. He kept coming." She burst into sobs. "So I shot him."

Judge Parden shook his head sadly, and after a long minute, Pasquale went on. "Tell us, please, where did you get the gun?"

"Doc gave it to me the day he went to Massachusetts. You know, the time when he got caught. He was going to meet with somebody about a drug deal, but I didn't know it then. He said he worried about me being alone. I said I didn't want it, but he made me take it anyway. We went outside, behind the house, and he showed me how to use it."

"Did you fire it yourself?"

"Yes. Once. He put a tin can on a fencepost and showed me how to use the gun. I held it with two hands. It made an awful noise, and it jumped when I pulled the trigger. I said I didn't want to do it again. He reloaded it, and I wrapped it in a towel and put it in the drawer next to the bed. I never touched it again until the night he came home."

Pasquale was finished, and Dean got to his feet. A red pimple had emerged on the end of his nose during the recess, and he dabbed it self-consciously as he walked to the stand.

"Mrs. O'Neil," he said, his voice jumping in and out of tune, "please tell us about your relationship with your husband before he went to jail. Did you love each other?"

"I did, and I thought he loved me. He knew I didn't approve of the business he was in. I tried to get him to stop, and when we moved to Maine, I thought maybe he'd take up something, well, you know, more respectable. He never did, but we got along just the same. I guess you could say we made a life."

Dean cut her off. "Would you describe your husband as a violent man?"

She hesitated. "He had a bad temper, and he got angry at me sometimes, but I couldn't say he ever hurt me. At the same time, I always knew there was a rage in him."

"Did you ever see him harm another person?"

"No, but I was never with him in his *other* life."

Dean changed the subject. "Now, I have to ask you about the kitchen knife. Don't you have any *real* cutting knives in your house?"

"I used to keep the good knives in a drawer, near the sink. For no particular reason, one day I moved them into the cupboard over the stove. This was after he went to jail. I guess he couldn't find them."

"Mrs. O'Neil," Dean asked carefully, "did you honestly believe he was going to harm you with an ordinary, dull table knife?"

Salome suddenly bristled. "Let me tell you, young man," she snapped, "if you'd been there and seen him, you'd run for your sorry ass."

Her response startled everybody, including Parden, who quickly jumped in. "Just answer the questions, Mrs. O'Neil," he said gently. She glanced at a scowling Pasquale, then heaved a sigh and nodded.

Dean gathered himself up and went on. "Let's talk a little bit about the money," he said. "I have to say, your testimony in this area does not make a whole lot of sense. Exactly what was your line of work when you met your husband?"

"I was a professional dancer, and a waitress."

Nibber snickered. Diane glared. "Shush!"

Dean bore down. "How did you support yourself while your husband was in prison?"

"I had some savings, and I took a job at Wal-Mart."

"That's it? Didn't you have a hard time making ends meet?"

Salome answered quickly. "The house was paid for. I got along just fine."

"Are you going to tell this court that you were not for one minute tempted by the money you claim your husband offered you?" Dean looked from Salome to the judge and back again. "According to your own testimony, you could have gotten your hands on a half-million dollars simply by going someplace and picking up a suitcase."

"I was not tempted," she said evenly. "It wasn't *my* money in the first place, and I knew there were lots of people who would come looking for it. Besides, that money is cursed."

"Cursed?" Dean looked surprised.

"Yes. It came from the sale of drugs. People had stolen, even died for it. Oh, it's cursed all right. You can be sure of that."

Harry slouched in his seat, and Dean pressed on. "But you wanted that money, didn't you?" He walked up close to the stand, wagging his finger.

"Not for a damn minute." Salome was getting upset again, and she was a match for the bullying.

"It was well worth killing for, wasn't it?"

"No, it wasn't."

Pasquale rose from his seat. "Objection! He's badgering. She's already answered those questions, more than once."

"Sustained." Parden was impatient.

"I have one final question," Dean leaned in. "On the day Mr. O'Neil showed you how to fire the gun," he asked, "did you hit the can on the fencepost?"

Salome gave a wry smile. "Nope," she said. "Missed by a mile."

The courtroom erupted again. The answer wasn't what Dean wanted to hear, and he made a quick swipe at the pimple and said he was done. Parden looked at the clock on the back wall. "Three thirty," he said. "I believe we have time to finish this up today. We'll take a short recess before closing arguments."

Salome stepped down and she and Pasquale went out the door behind the bench. The judge and Dean followed them. A buzz began to steadily build in the courtroom. "Where you puttin' your money?" Nibber asked, looking at Harry.

"Bad choice of words," Harry cautioned, "but I'm pretty sure she's going down."

"Oh no," Diane jumped back. "You couldn't have been watching the judge when Salome testified. I thought he might cry."

Debbie said she wasn't at all sure, and looked at Nibber, who slowly nodded his head. "My money's on Pasquale. He's some slick operator. Better get his telephone number. We might need him." Harry was about to reply when the back-room entourage returned and settled in.

Dean was first. "Your honor." He coughed and began again. "Your honor, this case is straightforward." He pointed at Salome, who had cleaned off the streaky mascara, re-painted her face, and was sitting chin high and chest out next to Pasquale. "This woman is a murderer."

Apparently given strength by his strong start, Dean's voice rose. "Mrs. O'Neil has admitted that her husband never put a hand on her all the time they were married, and we contend he never intended to hurt her on the night of March 7, either. He had no reason to. According to the defendant's own testimony, he already had the money. He didn't need to kill for something he already had. It makes no sense at all."

Dean glanced down at his notes. "The truth is, your honor, this woman had no feelings for her husband, hadn't bothered to visit him for nearly three years. She knew when he was coming home, and she knew he'd be carrying a suitcase full of money. She wanted that money, and so she went out and got hold of a .357 Ruger – with the serial numbers conveniently filed off, I might add – and laid in wait to kill him."

Harry heard Diane whisper. "*Lay* in wait."

"After she shot him in cold blood," Dean went on, "she went into the kitchen, found an ordinary table knife, and put it in his hand." He stopped, reached again for his handkerchief.

"Are you finished?" The judge glanced at the clock.

"Yes, your honor," Dean squeaked.

"Defense, please."

Pasquale picked up on Parden's impatience. "I will be brief," he said, smiling. "The long and short of it is that the prosecution's case is built entirely on cockamamie speculation about motive." He brought his belly within an inch of the bench. "I hope your honor will agree that the prosecution's case is seriously flawed on at least two major points. First, while we believe there is a pile of money somewhere, no one knows where it is now. Mr. Dean claims that Mrs. O'Neil killed for it, but Mrs. O'Neil doesn't have it. The prosecution certainly doesn't know where it is, or they would tell us. There are rumors that it is around here someplace, but so far, nobody has produced it." He paused, looked at Salome, then back to the judge. "Your honor, surely you will agree that in order to prove a charge of murder for money, there has to be at least a little money." Pasquale spread his hands, palms up. "Second, and most confusing to me," he continued, "the prosecution has failed to answer another important question related to its case, and that is if my client could have once had all that money without any trouble at all, why on earth would she wait three years and then murder for it?"

Pasquale went back to the table with Salome, and everyone in the courtroom sat staring at the judge, who looked down and fussed with the papers in front of him. Finally, he raised his head, removed his glasses and looked around the room. "Ordinarily," he said, "I would take such a case under advisement for a time, to review the facts and go over the transcript." He shook his head. "However, in this case I am certain that no amount of reflection will change my mind."

The only sound came from the birds, chirping outside the windows. "I have determined that Mrs. O'Neil shot her husband in self defense, and I find her not guilty of the charge of murder." He rapped the gavel and turned and smiled at Salome. "You are free to go, my dear."

Except for the hapless prosecutor, who gaped at the quickly vacated bench in disbelief, most everyone in the room began to applaud. Salome, sobbing in joy, latched onto Pasquale and rained kisses on his fat cheeks. Grandbush and poor Henry made a most peculiar couple as they embraced in the jury box, and down in front, the

Deacon and Molony carried on with whooping and high-fives. Debbie and Nibber did a jig in the aisle, and Diane grabbed Harry's hand. "You see," she whispered in his ear, "that money is good for something more than charity. It has set Salome free. Sweet justice has been done!"

Harry's eyes did a quick scan of the back of the courtroom. The Nurse was gone. "Maybe it has," he said, "and maybe it hasn't."

17

Quite by accident, Harry found himself trailing Nibber's Chevy on the ride to town. "Must be heading to work up at Falling Waters," he observed to Winston, who had figured things out for himself and was cavorting around the passenger seat, pausing on every turn to yelp a greeting out the window.

Except for the white smoke and fumes belching from Nibber's Chevy, the air was clear and filled with the fragrance of lilacs, and Harry was in high spirits until they reached the center of town where cars were clogging the narrow street. Horns blared and tires screeched as gaggles of tourists paraded back and forth across the road, walking over lawns, peering into windows. The first of the flatlanders had arrived for Memorial Day weekend, and the peace was gone.

As he neared the post office, Harry saw that a giant black SUV with New York plates had parked lengthwise out in front, blocking off the last two empty spaces. He whacked the steering wheel and seethed until he saw Nibber make a risky u-turn in front of Knight's and pull up nose-to-nose with the offending Goliath. Harry knew instantly what was up and edged his Toyota close to the rear bumper to complete the pen. "You wait," he said to Winston as he climbed out of the truck, "this'll be fun." Winston smirked.

Nibber was already rummaging through the post office wastebasket when Harry came in, and he nodded a greeting before he shouted over the boxes. "Mornin', Hummer. What's up?"

Hummer muted the ranting of Limbaugh and came to the open service window. "The town's in a buzz," he said, "and most of the racket is about the money."

Harry didn't want to hear it and turned to leave, but Nibber reached from the floor and grabbed his leg, motioning to the mailbox. "What money?" Nibber asked innocently.

"You know," the postmaster replied, "Doc's money."

"So what do ya hear?" Nibber wanted to know.

"Lots of loose cash floating around, everybody knows it. Somebody's making big donations in the cans across the road at Knight's, and sending some real handsome gifts through the mail."

"You don't say."

"It's true. But none of it's coming through this post office, else I'd know. They're being sent from up in Nice."

"Must be a nice person." Harry made a weak stab at changing the subject. Hummer didn't reply and went back to sorting. Nibber got off the floor with a fistful of coupons, and pointed out the window. "Oh, boy! Here he comes."

Harry looked. A short, bald-headed man was crossing the road, headed their way. "Wow!" Nibber observed. "This guy's got the planet covered – Bermuda shorts, Indian shirt, French sunglasses, and Jamaican sandals."

"Who owns the beater truck?" the man growled the instant he stepped inside.

Nibber stiffened. "Hold on, mister. I'm doin' you a big favor."

"Favor?" The red-faced man whipped off his French sunglasses.

"The sheriff was here a few minutes ago, looking for the owner of that SUV. Said she was going to write him up."

"Write him up? For what?"

"Oh, I dunno." Nibber rubbed his chin. "Said something about parking outside the lines, taking spaces reserved for post office patrons, exceeding the fifteen minute limit, stuff like that." Hummer was back at the service window, and looked on in amusement.

"Now, don't you worry yourself," Nibber said, patting the man's flowered shoulder. "The sheriff's a friend of mine. I told her your battery died, right there out front," he pointed. "Told her I had cables in the truck, and I'd be happy to pull up close and give you a good jump."

Hummer stifled a chuckle and went back to the boxes. The man paused, looked perplexed, and finally muttered an uncertain word of thanks. Nibber allowed as how it had been no trouble at all, and went out to move his Chevy. Hummer came outside, and the three watched as the man boarded the SUV, blew his horn at a hen mallard and her line of chicks in the road, and roared off toward the dam.

"You are bad," Harry said as he and Nibber crossed the street to Knight's where customers were bunched up in a semi-circle in front of the counter, elbowing one another for the chance to cash up.

"Let's skip the coffee," Nibber said disgustedly. "Don't any of 'em know they're supposed to be lining up on the left?"

"I suppose it's not their fault," Harry said. "No signs."

"We got no street signs, either," Nibber countered. "Don't need 'em, anyway. Everybody knows."

The two were about to leave when Nibber remembered he needed night crawlers. "Now you've got your boat in," he said, "I'm goin' fishing. Monday's a holiday. I get it off."

Harry turned back and got in line to the left, watching as grim-faced vacationers jostled one another for a chance to pay up and hurry off. He was thinking the scene could not be more depressing until he spied Jeff Molony, two places in front, holding an oozing red jelly doughnut and a cup of coffee. Molony saw him, set the doughnut on the counter, and pointed his free hand to the array of donation cans near the cash. "Look at that, will you?"

Harry looked. In the place where there were usually one, maybe two donation cans, this morning there were at least a half-dozen. He had begun to read the signs on the cans when Nibber returned with his tub of worms and gave Molony a chilly nod. "As you can see," Molony said, ignoring Nibber and pointing out the can collection to nearby customers, "everybody's trying to cash in on Belfry's eleemosynary eruption."

Nibber wrinkled his brow at Harry, who shrugged. The biggest container, a two-pound coffee can, was for Fourth of July fireworks. Harry nodded at Nibber. They'd agreed on that. Others, with hand-drawn labels pasted on, appealed for a variety of causes. A youngster on the East Road wanted to go to a pricey summer camp. A local horseshoe-pitching ace was looking for help to attend the world championships in Illinois, and Caleb Barnes had a plea for a prosthetic for a three-legged dog. Beneath Caleb's can was a referendum petition calling for the prohibition of deer-crossing signs on private property.

"That's stupid." Harry nodded at the petition sheet, already mostly filled up with signatures. "It'll never work."

"*That* won't work, either," Nibber said, putting a finger on the collection can.

"Why not?"

"Caleb doesn't have a dog."

Molony spotted John Knight and headed his way. John saw him coming and sidestepped behind the meat counter. Nibber returned and moved in line ahead of Harry, dumping the tub of crawlers on the counter next to Molony's jelly doughnut. Allie Knight caught him. "What in God's name are you doing?"

"Supposed to be a dozen worms in here," Nibber said, spreading out the moist dirt, counting. "One time last year I got only eleven."

"Good grief," Allie said, snatching up Molony's doughnut and putting a new one in a bag. "Here," she said, offering the exposed doughnut to Nibber, "give it to Winston."

Nibber put up his hand. "Winston doesn't much like jelly. Can I trade for a plain sugared?"

Outside, they lingered near the pumps, sharing Molony's contaminated doughnut that Nibber had retrieved from the trash. "Don't forget," Nibber said, wiping red jelly on his front, "Debbie's off at one, and we're going to meet at the dam. I've got a great surprise."

"I'm not sure I can take another one of your surprises." Harry spoke through the window of the rusty Chevy as Nibber revved the engine and created a temporary smoke screen that he used to edge his way back in traffic.

Harry headed his Toyota the other way, toward home, stopping along the way to chat with Chuck and Suzette Greaver, back from the Caribbean with handsome tans and out planting flowers in front of the Belfry Inn, readying for the Mother's Day opening. Up the road, Harry waved to Kerri Woods, whose Lake Lodge was nearly half full, the best it ever got. In the midst of several vehicles, Harry spotted the white pickup and did some quick figuring in his head. The Nurse was on at least his sixth visit since the night Doc got killed. He slowed down to see if there were any Vermont rental plates, but he couldn't be sure, and it kept him wondering until he got home.

Diane was seated at the kitchen table, left-handedly scrawling addresses on more Manila envelopes. "We have to make another withdrawal," she said without looking up.

Harry produced a flyer from the morning mail. "I've got another place for a drop," he said, going on to explain that the Humane Society in Watford needed help. Winston, who had been waltzing with Diane's slippers, let go of them and raised the corners of his long lips in a satisfied grin.

Harry gestured toward the envelopes. "We'll take this batch to Watford," he said. "Thanks to Hummer's big mouth, people have caught on to the drops in Nice." He thumbed through the envelopes she had finished – family violence prevention, hospice, the community college scholarship fund, and a few others. "This business of giving money away turns out to be quite tricky," he observed. "Almost everybody in Belfry is trying to guess who's got Doc's suitcase. It's like a big game of *Button, Button.*"

"Ah, don't worry," Diane said, gauging the weight of one of the envelopes before applying a strip of stamps. "We have to be extra careful, that's all."

Harry and Winston went off to the garage to make a withdrawal, and then Harry spent the rest of the morning in his upstairs office, going over Diane's meticulous donation ledger, kept in a shoebox in the back of the closet.

* * * *

At noon, Harry and Diane drove up to the dam to find out about Nibber's surprise, and when they pulled into the reserved Dam Committee parking spaces, Harry noticed that Molony had already put in his maze of docks below the spillway. "Just you wait," he said to Diane, "the water level won't suit him. He'll be squawking before the week is out."

"What's new?" Diane said as she wound down the window to give some air to Winston, who was slouched in the jump seat, grumbling about the cramped space.

"Don't get out!" The startling voice came through Harry's open window. It was Nibber. Debbie was standing next to him. "Stay right there," Nibber said, fumbling in his pocket. Within seconds there was a familiar whining sound, and the Tainter gate slowly began to rise.

"How on earth did you do that?" Harry was dumbfounded.

"Garage door opener." Nibber beamed.

"You didn't."

"I did. It was simple. All I had to do was connect the switch to the remote. Took fifteen minutes. Now, when it's raining, I can manage the dam from my truck." He reached through the window and hooked his finger in Harry's shirt. "And I still have the door motor. Maybe we should install it in your garage to improve security."

Diane laughed, and Debbie gave Nibber a fawn-eyed look. "Oh, Nibber, you are sooo clever."

Harry frowned, pushed Nibber's finger off his shirt. "I'm not at all sure this was a good idea," he said. "Your wizardry doesn't always work out."

"Like when?" Nibber demanded.

"Like your clapper toaster."

"Clapper toaster?" Diane didn't get it.

"Oh, well," Harry explained, "last year, he bought himself one of those sound activated switches they advertise on TV. Hooked it up to his toaster so he could clap for toast in bed in the morning. Doesn't work."

"Needs a stronger spring, that's all." Nibber jumped back. "And I've gotta figure out a way to have the toast arrive already buttered." He scratched his head. "Maybe I should just butter it up the night before."

"Some day, you'll burn down your cabin." Harry shook his head. "With our clapper toaster and all your *Playboys* in it."

Nibber pushed a button to re-set the gate before shoving the control back in his pocket, and all four headed off to the Sunrise where the good old boys already had a head start on the holiday weekend. All the stools along the bar were filled, and some were standing in back. In the very middle was Henry McLaughlin, who was at the moment waving to the bartender and ordering up a round for the house. Nibber headed straight for the bar.

"Hey there," Henry gushed real friendly like, pointing to his longneck, "have one on me." Nibber gave him a dirty look. Poor Henry looked sheepish. "Got a tax refund from the town," he explained. "Almost fifty bucks."

"You must have overpaid his taxes," Harry whispered to Diane when they were settled in their usual booth.

"Couldn't get a fix on the interest," she said as Debbie left to wait on customers, including Kelly Hallowell, seated alone at a table in the corner. Diane waved her over.

"So, what are you boys up to?" the deputy asked as she squeezed in next to Nibber.

"Well, for one thing," Nibber said, "we've been helping you out with traffic control around town." He went on at some length about the morning clearance of the SUV.

Kelly grinned at the tale, then turned serious. "Speaking of playing fast and loose with justice, what'd you guys think of the O'Neil trial?"

"I thought you were splendid," Diane said, reassuringly.

"I don't mean that," Kelly said, "but I must say, I think I did a pretty good job. It was my first time, you know."

"Not bad for a virgin," Nibber quipped.

Kelly ignored him. "No, I mean how do you feel about how everything came out?"

"I think they came out the way they were supposed to," Diane said.

Kelly shrugged. "I'm not so sure. There's something fishy about the whole thing."

Harry perked up. "You saying you don't think Salome shot Doc?"

"Maybe I am," Kelly answered. "I know Salome confessed, but I'm pretty good at reading people, as you know, and I just don't read her as being able to kill anybody, not even in self-defense."

"Neither do I," Nibber piped up. "I vote for the Nurse. He's got real killing experience."

Harry was stunned. He thought he was alone in his doubts and was surprised to find he had some company. "So," he said, "I suppose you two also have a theory on why Salome would take the fall for anybody, especially for the Nurse."

"Better than getting shot herself, I guess." Nibber had given it some thought.

"Tell you what," Harry turned back to Kelly, "if you have some doubts, there's nothing to keep you from doing a little investigating of your own. Might even make you a hero."

"A *heroine*," Diane cut in.

"It's not right to poke around after there's been a verdict." Kelly looked at Diane. "Besides, what's there to investigate?"

Harry was ready. "You could begin by checking out those two mystery men who keep coming and going from Kerri Woods' place. I'm pretty sure one of them is your top suspect. And, is the other guy really a cop? What could he tell you? And while you're at it, you might check on the phone calls that went in and out of the O'Neil house that night."

Nibber shot a puzzled look, said nothing.

"Oh, I'm not sure about *that*," Kelly said slowly. "You'd need a warrant to check phone records."

"Not if you used to work at the phone company and still have friends there." Harry pushed.

Kelly paused, sipped her Coke. "Maybe I will," she said.

They hadn't ordered, but Debbie came to the table with their meals just the same. "The usual," she said putting down salads for Harry and Diane and ceremoniously placing a dish of meat loaf in front of Nibber before handing him a freshly filled catsup bottle and a lobster bib. "I'll join you when things slow down."

They ate and chatted. Nibber pumped Kelly about several local cases of petty crime, but she was in uniform and wouldn't talk about anything except the missing suitcase. "Mal Grandbush says Aidan Brown has it," she said, out of the blue.

"Not likely," Diane dismissed the idea.

"Turns out, I agree," Kelly said, leaning over and lowering her voice. "If you ask me, she's making up the story because she's got the damned suitcase herself."

Nibber spewed a speck of meatloaf. "How you figure?"

"Last month she's crying poor mouth at Town Meeting, saying we can't have a new library for a long time. Next thing you know, she's around blabbing that a new library's in sight. What's changed? The town hasn't coughed up any money, and fund-raising has been a bust. I think she's got the suitcase and plans to pay for the job herself."

Kelly's satisfying theory hung in the smoky air for a long time until her two-way radio squawked, and she wiggled her way out of the booth and went outside to answer. She was back in seconds, waving her arms. "Come with me!" she yelled. "The dam's wide open!"

Debbie ran out of the kitchen to join the others, and they raced out the door with the rest of the Sunrise crowd close behind. Nibber's truck was nearest the road, and all four piled in and headed up the road behind Kelly's cruiser, its siren screaming.

"For God's sake, take it easy, will you?" Diane yelled from the jump seat. "Debbie and I are sitting on a come-along back here."

Flatlanders scattered as they zipped through Main Street, screeching to a halt on the bridge over the dam. The Tainter gate was indeed wide open, its jaw higher than Harry had ever seen, and a big crowd had gathered on the banks, gaping and cheering at the astonishing, boiling rush of water into Finger Lake.

Nibber jumped out of the truck, all the while frantically thumbing at the new remote control. In a second or two, the gate began to slowly close. "I think I know what went wrong," he said, looking down.

"Me, too." Harry was disgusted. "You put the clicker in your pocket and sat on it when we left the dam."

Nibber seemed remorseful as he unlocked the chain to the catwalk, and all four moved out to watch the gate make its painfully slow descent. The fun was over, and the crowd evaporated almost as quickly as it had formed.

Harry surveyed the spillway. The far wall was tilting a bit more toward the water, but otherwise there was little damage. His eyes followed the full length of the wall, and he spotted a rowboat a hundred yards off shore. "Look here," he said, pointing. "It's Molony." Even though the gate had been open for only a couple of hours, the great rush of water had lifted the wooden decking of Molony's docks up and out of their frames, sending them in a long, northbound convoy up Finger Lake.

All four listened to Molony cursing above the howling water as he flailed at the oars, rocking the tiny boat from side to side in the effort to coral the wayward decking and tow it all to shore. The scene sent Debbie and Diane into gales of laughter. Nibber looked at Harry and stifled a grin. "Let's go," he said. "We don't any of us want to be here when Bolony comes ashore."

18

The lawn at Falling Waters bristled with volunteers who had gathered up for the final Saturday morning renovation muster. Assorted pickups lined the long church driveway, and a dozen men stood around the cherry picker, listening as Gus Gammon gave instructions on how they would put the old bell into the new belfry. On the front steps, women chattered as they sorted pails and mops in preparation for giving the sanctuary a good scrubbing.

"Where's Diane?" Nibber got to his feet after a slurpy reunion with Winston.

"Under the weather, I'm afraid." Harry explained. "Been going on a week or more, but she usually feels better by noon. Said to be sure to tell you tonight's celebration of the sale of Debbie's house is still on. Our place. At five."

"I wish she was here right now," Nibber said, pointing to the movable letter sign on the lawn behind them.

Joyful Waters Is Rising
Easter Coming - July 4th

Harry agreed. "There's a whole lot for her to fix on that."

"The man's a flat-out whacko," Nibber muttered, "but I've warmed to him since the renovations began."

"Me, too," Harry said, "but then again, I've always had a soft spot for nut cases."

Nibber missed the point. "When you think about it," he said, "this whole town's filled with nut cases. Right now, they're working extra shifts at the rumor mill, churning out suitcase suspects. There's been even more since Diane's last drop."

"Let's see," Harry counted on his fingers. "Mal Grandbush says she's pretty sure Aidan Brown has it. Kelly Hallowell claims it's Mal Grandbush. John Knight is certain Jeff Molony is funding his real estate deals with it. That's three. And, here's one even you haven't heard. Gus Gammon took me aside at the mill yesterday and said he was troubled about having Henry McLaughlin on the Joyful Waters payroll. Seems he thinks poor Henry is the one with the suitcase."

"Poor Henry? That's freakin' crazy."

Harry shrugged. "Hard to argue with the old guy. Think about it. Here, we've got a penniless man who all of a sudden ups and pays his back taxes and starts buying rounds of beer at the Sunrise. I'd say he makes a good suspect."

Nibber cocked his head, and Harry suddenly realized his friend was actually thinking about the possibility that poor Henry had the case. Nibber had become so wrapped up in the community guessing game that he sometimes forgot who actually had the damn thing.

Harry reminded him. "I'd say we're darn lucky nobody's put the finger on us." He paused, then added. "Yet."

"Don't be so sure." Nibber's face grew serious. "If we were on the list, we'd be the last to know. Mal's on it, and she doesn't know. Course she's dropped down a bit since the town announced its plan to buy the Swift farm, but her name is still getting bandied about."

It's true, Harry thought. When the *Watford Journal* made a big splash on the town's decision to acquire Debbie's farm, it carried a separate story on the proposal of including the new library in the project. Since then, fewer people had been tying Mal to the suitcase.

"Anyway, I'm fine with all the rumors," Harry said. "They keep the spotlight off us. I just worry about the things that *are* true, and the truth is the Nurse and what's-his-name, agent Hemphill, are still prowling around two months after Doc got shot."

"Hemphill's the right name," Nibber said, "but it's funny we've never seen him. Just his car, and he keeps changing that." He looked up. "By the way, I completely forgot to tell you that John Knight asked me yesterday if I knew the man with the scar on his cheek, driving a white pickup and staying now and then at Kelly's lodge."

"Figures." Harry shrugged.

"Ah, but the reason he wanted to know was because the Nurse has been asking questions about the money."

"You're not kidding?"

"Nope. John claims he started out by asking about the donation cans."

"Well, that doesn't surprise me. These days, there are so many cans that Allie's had to put a card table in front of the counter to handle 'em all."

"Anyway," Nibber went on, "John knows all the theories about who might have the money, but the Nurse being a flatlander and all, he said he didn't feel comfortable sharing any rumors."

"This thing is giving me the heebie-jeebies," Harry said, pawing the grass with his feet. "We've really gotta get serious about finding a better place to hide the suitcase."

"You're right," Nibber replied. "And, I been thinkin' about it."

"And?"

"Still thinkin'," Nibber said as they turned to watch old man Gammon direct the cherry picker up close to the front door of Falling Waters. Peppard had been inside and must have heard the back-up beeper, because he squeezed sideways out the door in the nick of time.

"This is the day the Lord has made," the preacher proclaimed, raising his stubby arms and beaming as he stood beside the grounded bell.

"Muffle it!" Nibber spoke sharply, then caught Peppard's astonished look. "The bell," Nibber expanded. "Muffle the bell, so it won't clang when we lift it."

Several men attached chains to the bell, and while the rest waited, Molony shuffled over. "Tell me," he asked, avoiding Nibber and looking directly at Harry, "why on earth do you think Debbie Swift sold her farm to the town instead of me? The price I offered was the same."

Harry considered it a fair question, and wished he were better prepared. "Well?" Molony was impatient.

Nibber seemed eager to fill the breach. "Two reasons," he said calmly, his jaw in Molony's face. "First, because she doesn't want the farm to be cut up in little pieces, and second, because she knows the town would never screw her."

Molony raised a fist; his eyes shot fire. Harry jumped between the two, and Molony stepped back, quivering. After an awkward pause, he turned in a huff and stalked back to the Deacon, who had been doing his best to overhear.

"Hey, take it easy," Harry said when Molony was gone. "The man's been mad enough since the episode with the dam clicker. No sense to rile him any more. Besides, this bell job's gonna take all the hands we can get." Nibber nodded, but didn't appear sorry, and Harry hid a tiny smile as the two moved off to join the queue at a ladder propped up on the church wall.

Safely perched on the roof with the rest of the crew, Harry looked down onto the lawn and saw the Deacon and Molony, hands in their pockets, schmoozing with Peppard. "So much for getting all hands on deck," he observed to Nibber, whose eyes were fixed near the front door where old man Gammon had attached the chains to the picker claw and was slowly beginning the lift.

The heavy load came up easily enough, but it took several tries before the men were able to pull the bell the last few horizontal feet and onto the hook. It took two hours or more, and when they were done, the men sat like crows along the ridgepole, slapping high-fives and cheering.

Nibber took a minute to catch his breath, and then reached to remove the burlap from the clapper and tie a rope to the bell crank. He dropped the end of the rope through the small hole in the roof and into the vestibule below, and scrambled down the ladder and through the front door. He was about to give the bell a test yank when Peppard appeared from nowhere and reached out to stop him.

"Wait," the preacher said. "Bad luck. We'll re-consecrate it July 4th, and then we can ring it. I'll get the Knight kid to do it. You know, the one who dropped the marble and gave the sign." He shrugged. "I misread it of course, but it was a sign just the same."

Nibber grinned, gave Peppard a gentle slap on the back and headed outside where Harry and the others were looking up, admiring their work. Nibber shook hands all around. "That's it for today," he said. "No heavy work left. I'll close the side of the belfry next week, and re-set the pews after that. We'll be done for the Fourth."

Peppard insisted on leading a prayer of thanksgiving, and when most everybody was gone, followed Harry and Nibber inside for an inspection. The refinished pews were stacked high on the back wall, and the empty sanctuary floor gleamed from the final coat of new varnish. The women had washed the windows, dusted the sills, and polished the cross on the altar.

"Isn't it wonderful?" Peppard gushed as Thelma McCracken removed her shoes and tiptoed carefully toward the old upright. "Had it tuned for her," the pastor said proudly, "as a surprise." The piano legs had been blocked up an inch or two to let the varnish dry, and when she sat down to practice Peppard's chosen re-consecration hymn in her bare feet, she seemed to Harry to be smaller than ever. He moved closer and watched a broad smile spread over her face as she pecked out a halting but finely tuned verse of the vaguely familiar hymn *Life is Brief and Full of Trouble*.

Harry looked at his watch. "Gotta go home," he said, "and get ready for the party."

"Me, too," Nibber said. "I'll borrow Winston. We have things to discuss."

Harry rode home alone and barely had time to change his clothes when Winston galloped through the door with Nibber and Debbie close behind. Winston greeted Diane as if he'd been gone for a month, and all four went onto the porch for salsa, tortilla chips, and an unofficial meeting of the Dam Committee, plus one.

Harry toasted with a Sam Adams. "Here's to the sale of the Swift Farm," he said, "and to Debbie's future." He clicked on Nibber's can of Bud, Debbie's white Zin, and Diane's tall glass of ice water. "And while we're at it," he added, "let's hoist one for Nibber, who is certain to have Joyful Waters ready for the Fourth of July, as promised." They all clicked again.

"Speaking of the Fourth of July," Diane said, "Allie told me at Knight's this morning that we're set to have the biggest fireworks show Belfry's ever seen. They've collected more than twice as much money as they ever did before." She giggled. "Of course, the five hundred I put in didn't hurt."

"*You* put in five hundred?" Harry's eyes went wide. "So did I."

Nibber waited for the laughing to stop. "Me, too."

"Goodness me," Diane said, "from now on, nobody makes a drop unless I record it first. We'll start the new system now, beginning with the Watford Humane Shelter. Five hundred is suggested. I'll send it. Plain envelope. All in favor?" The others raised their hands, and an approving yip came from the floor in front of Nibber's chair, where Winston waited for bits of flying tortillas.

"I believe it's time to be thinking about repeat giving," Diane suggested. "We seem to have run the gamut. How about doing Joyful Waters and the Belfry Library again? Thanks to us, they both seem to be on the right track. And maybe another grant to the soup kitchen, to help stock up for the fall." All agreed.

Harry changed the subject. "Nibber says he's been thinking about a new place to hide the money."

"About time," Diane said, looking at Nibber.

"Still thinkin'," he said as he gazed out over the lake.

"And another thing," Harry skipped over the suitcase. "I talked with Kelly Hallowell this morning when she stopped at Joyful Waters to direct traffic around the picker. Said she'd done some checking on the two mystery men, but came up empty. She allowed as how one of them is probably a federal agent and the other's a former partner of Doc's. We already knew that. So did she. That would be the Hemphill and the Nurse. Says she thinks both are here looking for the suitcase."

"So what's new?" Nibber shrugged.

"Nothing at all on that front," Harry admitted, "or the phone calls either, but Kelly did say she's giving serious thought to asking her friend at the phone company to slip her the records. That's progress."

"Makes me think," Diane jumped in. "Has anybody seen Salome? I wonder how she's doing."

"She's doin' just fine," Nibber said. "I was at the O'Neil house yesterday, putting the last coat of paint on the wall back of the stair landing. Smooth as silk. Not a trace of Doc."

"Yuk!" Debbie buried her nose in her Zin.

"The Deacon was there," Nibber added. "Said he was just leaving when I got there. Told me Salome's mother died and he'd come to give comfort."

"Well, at least we know her mother was really sick," Harry said. "I wondered."

Diane slipped into the kitchen, and called back. "Supper's ready." Nibber had caught a large Brown trout and given it, un-cleaned, to Diane. It was his first contribution to the Crockett larder in a long time, and it made him proud, so proud in fact that the fish grew in length and weight every time he brought it up.

Harry watched Diane admiringly as she took Nibber's gift out of the oven, garnished it with parsley and lemon wedges, and put the platter next to a bowl of the season's first peas. The table was set with fine linen, China plates, and sterling. "Pretty special," he said.

"Special all around," Diane replied, carefully covering the trout's head with a paper napkin before ceremoniously placing two envelopes in front of Harry's plate.

"What's this?" He looked puzzled.

"Tomorrow is Father's Day." She wore a broad grin.

"A card from Winston," Harry explained to the others. "Diane never forgets. But, what's the other one?"

Diane glanced around the table, and then looked directly at Harry. "Went to the doctor's in Watford yesterday." The words tumbled out. "He told me you're going to have to give up your office upstairs. We're going to have a baby!"

Harry sat stunned, and after a few seconds, a big smile came over his face. His eyes welled with tears. Debbie rushed to give Diane a hug, and Nibber leaped to his feet, knocking over his can of Bud as he paraded around the table with Winston.

When the loud celebration finally stopped, Harry got up, walked slowly to Diane's chair and put his arms around her neck. "I swear," he choked, "I'm never going to worry about another thing so long as I live." He bent to hug her. "Except you and the baby." A tear ran slowly down his cheek, and he laughed when he wiped it away. "And Nibber, of course."

19

The Fourth of July dawned sizzling hot, and Nibber sat sweating with the others in a front pew of Joyful Waters. Dark circles formed in the armpits of his Dam Committee T-shirt as he greeted a steady trickle of admiring parishioners, gathering up for the morning re-consecration.

"We barely finished the job," Nibber said during a lull in the handshaking. "Debbie came up after work, and we screwed in the pews until well after midnight."

"Oh, good Lord!" Diane raised her eyes to the newly repaired stained glass window behind the altar. "Neither commas nor spelling will save us. We must pray for entirely new words."

Harry had caught on, and he fed Nibber a line. "Was Peppard here, too?"

Nibber ran with it. "Oh, yes, he was here, all right," he grinned. "Didn't help at all, but he really enjoyed watching."

"Okay, boys," Diane said, "that will be quite enough."

Debbie blushed and promptly changed the subject. "I hope this re-consecrating business doesn't take too long," she said. "It's much too warm to be inside, and the parade starts at ten."

Harry, who had been in a lighter mood since learning he was going to be a father, had a momentary relapse. "These seats way up front are terrible."

"Can't do anything about it," Diane explained for the second time, pointing to a hand-lettered placard Peppard had carefully taped to the end of the front pew: *Mr. Nabroski & Friends.*

Harry craned his neck to look behind. The place was nearly full, mostly with regulars but the worshipers included a fair number of flatlanders, women in flowered dresses and broad-brimmed straw hats, men in chinos with penny loafers and no socks. He was about to turn back to the front when he spotted a familiar figure sashaying through the door. "Have a look at that," he said, giving Diane a nudge.

Salome O'Neil, wearing a short skirt and a bravely open red blouse, stood under the archway and glanced furtively around the crowded pews. Molony and the Deacon had just finished several ushering trips with the Knight family and their countless kids when they spotted her. The long-legged Deacon won the two-man race to the door.

"A coming-out party," Harry said as the fawning Deacon chatted with Salome before finding her a place next to Mal Grandbush, who welcomed her in, visibly delighted at having Belfry's most intriguing woman as a morning seatmate.

"Come now," Diane said, "Salome's trying to make a new life for herself. We should be supportive."

"I'm not at all sure she needs much help," Harry replied, just as Peppard entered from behind the altar. The hefty pastor had manufactured his own vestments for the occasion, and his regular robe was stitched from shoulders to hem with wide, horizontal bands of red, white and blue cotton. Glittering tinfoil stars were glued here and there on his favorite loon stole.

"Put a rocket under that," Nibber quipped, "and we'd have ourselves a real old fashioned Fourth."

"Shush!"

Harry thought the ceremony was mercifully brief. Peppard began by making it clear the Lord had entered the sanctuary right behind him, and then, looking a match for the famous Uncle Sam poster, pointed his finger here and there into the assembly and began thanking volunteers. He called off a few of the most faithful renovators by name – Harry, Gus Gammon, poor Henry, and one or two others – then heaped singular praise on "Brother Nabroski for his great sacrifice in leading the resurrection of Joyful Waters." Nibber turned to acknowledge the applause and stayed on his feet while wizened Thelma enthusiastically accompanied the congregation in three full verses of *See Him Walk on the Water*.

"A bit over the top, I'd say," Harry muttered when the singing stopped.

"Yes, indeed," Nibber beamed.

Peppard ended with a longish re-dedication prayer and then walked slowly up the aisle, waving his arms and blessing every corner. When he reached the door, he tilted his head skyward and in a loud voice asked the Lord to make the old bell ring. The Deacon, standing stiffly by the door, took the cue and made an ill-disguised hand signal into the vestibule where the Knight kid of marble fame began pulling the rope with all his might. The clanging all but drowned out the recessional, and most everybody plugged their ears as they made their way out past the bobbing youngster, who rode a foot or two off the floor on every backswing of the heavy bell.

* * * *

Parade marshal Durwood Green, wearing his karaoke tux, did his best to line up the units in the Grange parking lot, and Kelly Hallowell blew her whistle and waved a nightstick as she sorted out a snarl of antique cars and fleeing flatlanders.

Nibber said he and Debbie would walk up the road and watch the parade from the sidewalk near the Sunrise. "So she won't have to fight traffic and be on time for work," Nibber explained. "She's off again at seven," he said to Harry as they left. "If you don't mind, I'd like to take your boat to Loit's Island. We'll have a picnic and watch the fireworks from there. You're welcome to join us if you want."

Harry was about to accept when Diane jumped in. "You two have a good time by yourselves," she said. "We'll stay at home, watch the show from the porch." Harry, uncertain whether Diane was protecting Debbie or her own delicate condition, grabbed her hand, and the two made their way across the sun-parched lawn.

When they reached the road, Harry looked back at the re-born and plumb-straight church, its freshly painted white clapboards gleaming in the sun. "We've done something good with bad money," he said, solemnly.

Diane nodded in agreement just as the fire station siren wailed the signal for the parade to begin. They ran the last few yards to the bridge and squeezed in next to Susan Woods, who pointed toward a large barge, anchored in the stream above the dam. Several men were arranging canisters along the deck, preparing for the night's fireworks. "Just you wait 'til you see *this* show," the town manager said. "We got an unbelievable amount of donations. It was like Santa Claus came three times." Harry stole a sideways glance at Diane. "Just look at the biggest can," Woods went on, pointing toward the barge. "They won't have a better finale on the Charles in Boston."

She was set to elaborate when Aidan Brown's cruiser crept slowly over the bridge, all blue lights and beeping, clearing spectators who scurried into lawn chairs and onto fenders and roofs of cars that lined both sides of the road. Behind the cruiser, the honorary grand marshal Peppard, still in his Uncle Sam garb, waved an American flag from his seat on a bale of straw in the back of the Deacon's army Jeep. The Deacon was driving with one hand, waving with the other. Molony mimicked his sidekick on the passenger side, bobbing and smiling.

A sudden burst of wild cheering startled Harry, but then he realized the howling was not for the holy trio, but for Darlene Ruff, next in line, leading a cadre of horses from the Belfry Riding Club. Sitting tall in the saddle of a bouncing Appaloosa, her once-blond hair fell in curls down the front of a shimmering red, sequin-covered, two-piece bikini.

Diane watched Harry gape. "Lady Godiva on the Fourth of July," she said. "Must be our founding mother."

Harry grinned and gawked until Darlene had gotten by, then pointed to the pavement, littered with droppings. "Having the horses in front was not a good idea," he observed as a frazzled den mother ran back and forth across the road, trying in vain to steer her excited cubs around the poop.

Mal Grandbush trailed the scouts, ignoring the steaming land mines and keeping a steady course along the yellow centerline, wagging a cardboard sign proclaiming the virtues of reading. Poor Henry, who had been watching from the sidewalk, suddenly popped in line behind her and, keeping his head down, did his best to follow Mal along the painted line. Caleb Barnes, the last of the unregistered entries, marched proudly by himself, carrying an uprooted deer crossing sign.

The rest of the parade order was the same as always. Knight's Store had dusted off last year's float, and the uncountable Knight kids hung over the rails and tossed hard candy into the crowd. Chuck and Suzette Greaver pulled a papier mâché duck in a red cart to advertise the

Belfry Inn, and old man Gammon drove a flatbed, covered with bunting and filled with youngsters from Belfry Elementary, playing *Yankee Doodle* on their kazoos. Bringing up the rear, just in front of Belfry's 1954 Seagraves pumper, were the Shriners, old men in fezzes driving noisy motorized go-carts in dizzying patterns around and through the droppings.

When the parade was over, Harry and Diane walked the length of the crowded Main Street, taking in the sights. The air was filled with the smells of fried dough and hotdogs, and the sidewalks on both sides were crammed with vendors selling all manner of local products, from whoopee pies to turkey burgers.

"Let's skip the loon-calling contest," Diane said as they passed an array of Elvis portraits on velvet. "I'm weary."

Harry looked away from a card table piled with discounted macramé coat hangers. "Fine with me," he said, putting an arm around her waist as they made their way back up the road to find the truck.

20

They sat on the front porch, sipping lemonade and peering over the steamy lake, crawling with party boats and screaming jet-skis. Winston crouched on the floor between them, paws over his ears, wincing at the snap of firecrackers and the eerie wails of loon imitators carrying over the water from the dam.

Diane looked at the trembling dog and shook her head. "I wonder how he's ever going to accept the new baby," she said. "He doesn't like changes of any sort, and he certainly doesn't like to be ignored. He was in a bad mood when we got back from the parade. I've never heard such words out of a dog's mouth."

The air split with the explosion of a cherry bomb down the shore, and Harry waited for the echoes to stop before he answered. "He'll be just fine," he said. "The one I worry about is Nibber."

"Nibber?" Diane looked surprised. "When a baby's coming, people usually worry more about their other kids than their dogs." She thought for a second. "Well, I get your point. We'll just have to get Nibber involved in some way. Maybe he can help restore the nursery."

"Speak of the devil." Harry cupped an ear toward the rattle and backfiring of Nibber's Chevy in the driveway. "He's come to get the boat."

Nibber burst onto the porch and flopped on the floor with Winston, who quickly turned on his back, looking for sympathy. "There's fish blood in the bottom of the boat and dried worms on the gunnels," Nibber said. "I'll clean it all up at the marina. Debbie's comin' to meet me after work, with a picnic."

Harry's eyes lit up, and Diane was quick. "We can't leave Winston," she said. "He'll be apoplectic when the fireworks show begins."

"Apoplectic?" Nibber repeated over his shoulder as he walked down to the dock. "I guess we can't have any of that." Diane laughed, and they watched as he untied the boat and motored slowly down the lake, weaving in and out to avoid speedboats hauling tubes filled with yelling kids.

Diane picked up the earlier thought. "Nibber will be just fine," she said. "His work is done at Falling Waters, but he's got a few odd jobs lined up. And besides, he's got Debbie. Both of them are a lot better off since we got the suitcase."

"And so are we." Harry smiled and patted her belly. "Now all we have to do is keep the vultures at bay, find a safer place for the suitcase, and figure out what to do with the rest of the money."

* * * *

They talked on through the afternoon, planning the nursery and tossing around ideas for new money drops. Soon after seven, they waved to Nibber and Debbie as they putted by, heading out to Loit's Island. Winston scampered down to the dock, expecting an invitation, but Diane called him back with the promise of a special treat, and went inside to fix it.

"What's that you're reading?" she asked when she returned with sandwiches, lemonade, and a fistful of raw carrots.

"The gun show catalogue the Deacon made me take the day I went to pick him up."

"You don't like guns."

"No, but there's a picture in here of a Ruger, like the one Salome used. I just wanted to have a close look."

"A Ruger is a Ruger, I suspect," Diane said.

"Maybe," Harry said, picking up his head to watch across the way as several boats began to anchor at the mouth of Mosher Stream to await the show.

Winston, finished with the carrots, stretched out on the floor, watching cross-eyed as a fly walked idly over his nose. Harry went inside to get bug spray and a bed pillow.

Darkness came a few minutes after nine, and the show began on time with the giant eruption of cannon that launched a half-dozen rockets, trailing red, white, and blue, and streaming out in every direction over the lake. The booms continued, one after the other, and Diane shrieked at each new display – Roman candles and repeaters, wagon wheels and waterfalls. Winston cringed at every explosion. Harry bunched the pillow over his head.

The aerial shelling went on for a long time, and just as Harry was about to proclaim that it was the grandest display Belfry had ever seen, the ground trembled with a mighty roar, and they watched in amazement as a giant, flame-spewing mortar roared straight up into the smoke-filled sky. Harry thought maybe the raging missile would simply disappear out of sight when there came a second, ear-splitting explosion, and the rocket suddenly reversed direction and headed in a long arc out over the water. In an instant, they both realized the ball of fire was headed straight for Loit's Island. "Oh my God!" Diane put her hand up to her mouth. "Debbie and Nibber!"

They rushed to the porch rail and craned their necks just in time to see the blazing rocket land in a spray of sparks on the near shore of the island. Within seconds, the resounding thump carried over the water and they could see tiny plumes of white smoke drift into the sky. Boats parked in the stream began pulling anchors, revving engines, and forming a convoy, headed toward the island. Harry went to grab a flashlight and then ran to the dock where he waved to the Belfry Fire Department rescue boat as it pulled out of the marina.

"Help me," he yelled when they got closer. "My boat's out there somewhere." He gestured toward the island. "I need a lift." They heard and swung close to pick him up.

Bo Chilton, the road commissioner, was at the helm. "Easter Bunny's to blame for all of this," he harrumphed as Harry hopped aboard. "Never should have spent all that money on fireworks. They're gonna burn the place

down, and just to please the gawdamn flatlanders."
Harry nodded, remembering where a good part of the
money had come from, then turned to watch the man in
the bow, dressed in a bathing suit and a fire hat as he
directed a high-powered searchlight and waved Chilton
around boatloads of gawkers, running without lights.

As they neared the island, Harry spotted his empty
boat, its painter drooping in the water, drifting some fifty
yards from shore. Nibber and Debbie were nowhere in
sight, and Harry's heart went into his throat. He tapped
Chilton on the shoulder, gesturing toward his boat. "Put
me aboard," he said. He waited while Chilton rafted the
two boats together, just long enough for Harry to make
the jump.

The engine in Harry's boat started with a single pull,
and he headed in, nosing the bow onto a gravel patch
below the fire before he tied the line to a tree near the
water. Grabbing the branches of overhanging alder
bushes to keep his footing on the slippery rocks along the
shore, he played his flashlight in front and could see that
some of the early arrivals had already formed a bucket
brigade and were beginning to douse the flames. As he
came to a short stretch of sandy bottom, a harsh sound
came from the dense undergrowth to his left.

"Pssst!"

Harry spun his flashlight toward the sound, and in
the thick alders, made out the figure of a man, stark
naked, hands over his crotch.

"It's me," the voice squeaked. "Nibber."

Harry was relieved. "Yes, I can plainly see," he chuckled and turned off the flashlight.

"Bring the clothes!" Nibber's voice pleaded. "They're in the boat."

Harry waded out and found a bundle he hadn't noticed, under the bow seat. When he returned, eager hands reached through the undergrowth to grab it. A minute later, Nibber and Debbie appeared on the shore, fully dressed. Harry turned on the flashlight. Nibber was wearing a sheepish grin. Debbie seemed to be blushing.

The rocket fire was all but out, but here and there tiny trails of smoke filled the air with the sharp smell of burning duff. "We're okay now," Chilton announced up ahead to the tired crowd of volunteers, "but we've got an underground going on here. You people can leave. We'll stay and soak it out."

Harry waited with Nibber and Debbie until the first responders had gone, then all three climbed aboard Harry's boat and fell in line behind the rest, headed for the mainland. Harry was full of questions, but he knew better than to shout above the engine. His voice would carry all the way to shore. As he followed the lights to shore, he gazed in the dim light at Debbie, huddled in the bow, shivering, and Nibber, with a shit-eating grin, facing Harry from the middle seat.

Winston met them at the dock, and danced in circles as he trailed them to the house. Debbie ran upstairs for a shower, and Diane went to the stove to boil water for tea. Harry and Nibber sat alone at the table.

"For the love of Pete, what was going on out there?" Harry finally blurted, peering intently at Nibber.

"Well, to begin with, we were all by ourselves," Nibber began. "It was really nice. Had a fine picnic – chicken sandwiches, deviled eggs ..."

"Never mind the menu."

"After, we sat on the rocks. The sun was hot. Debbie said we should go swimming, but we didn't have suits."

Harry thought he knew where things were headed. "Honestly," Nibber went on as if he could read Harry's thoughts, "it was Debbie who suggested skinny dipping."

"And you objected, of course."

"Nope." Nibber smirked. "She took off her clothes, dropped them in the bottom of the boat, and jumped in the water, quick as that. I tried not to look. Really, I did."

Harry glanced up at Diane, back to, tending the kettle. Her shoulders were shaking. She was giggling.

"I put my clothes with hers and pulled the boat up on shore. I thought I'd tied it good."

"Obviously not."

"We swam around for awhile, watched the sun go down. After that, we went up on that tiny spit of sand near where you found us." Nibber hesitated, and then shrugged. "You see, one thing led to another. You know how it is." He stared at Harry, then let it out: "We did it."

"It?"

"You know. *It!*"

Diane's shoulders shook harder.

"Good lord!" Harry was digesting it all.

"Pretty soon, the fireworks started."

"I should say."

"The finale was something else."

"I'll bet."

"That rocket seemed to be coming straight at us. I could tell it was going to land close by and I ran to get our clothes, but the boat was gone. I could see it drifting out there, not far away. I was about to swim out and get it when the other boats started coming. We hid in the bushes. That's where you found us."

Nibber put his hands around the warm cup of tea. Winston, who hadn't budged once through the whole story, was gaping at Nibber in astonishment.

"So," Harry finally asked, "will the two of you be getting married?" It seemed an obvious question, but Nibber looked surprised.

"Jeezum, Harry. I told you we went all the way, but we didn't go *that* far."

21

It was well into August, and Harry was annoyed that he hadn't seen much of Nibber since the Fourth of July escapade on Loit's Island. He mentioned it to Diane at breakfast, but she wasn't at all helpful. "After his fine job at Falling Waters," she explained, "he's had more odd jobs than he can take care of, and since we put a moratorium on suitcase drops for awhile, there's been no need for meetings. Besides all that," she added, "you've got to take into account the matter of his new romance."

"We took care of him long before Debbie," Harry sulked.

"Indeed we did," Diane agreed, "and now you should be grateful you don't have to chaperone those two any more, not to mention the savings on groceries."

Harry still wasn't convinced, and now, as he and Winston headed off to the post office, he decided to drive up to Nibber's cabin and set things straight.

Winston seemed to think it was a fine idea, and when they reached the corner of Shore Drive and the spur leading up to the cabin, the dog jumped from the shotgun seat, vaulted into Harry's lap, and yapped in delight out the driver-side window. Harry brushed the bushy tail away from his face and yanked the Toyota into low gear to make the turn.

It had rained most of the month, and heavy thunderstorms had gully-washed Nibber's steep driveway. Harry paid close attention as he inched up the hill, and it wasn't until Nibber's cabin came into view that he noticed things were terribly wrong. The entire yard was picked up and neatly raked, and near the woods, a large pile of brush was set for burning. The timber chain-fall teepee and the old parts truck were gone, as was the collection of wrecked snowmobiles.

Harry gaped in amazement as he pulled up close to the cabin and got out. Winston ran up onto the porch where the usual clutter of cans, bottles, and boxes had disappeared. The porch floor was newly painted, and a hand-printed card was neatly taped to the screen: **Please Remove Your Shoes.**

Winston looked down at his paws before nosing through the door. Harry followed in his stocking feet. Inside, it was more of the same. The sink and sideboard were clear of dirty dishes, and the cupboard doors were scrubbed and evenly closed. Books lined the shelves like soldiers, the braided rug was clean and straight, and the haze was gone from the TV screen. Harry looked at his friend, niblessly seated at the freshly polished kitchen table, working on his checkbook. "What's goin' on here?" Harry asked, hunching his shoulders in amazement.

"Debbie, that's what."

"She's moved in?"

"Yup. Farm's been transferred to the town. They said she could stay on awhile, but with all the architects and contractors running around, there's no privacy. I invited her to move in here last month, not long after the Fourth, but it's taken us some time to get the place straightened up."

"She's doin' the cooking?"

Nibber yupped again. "And she's about cleaned out the freezer. Came across Wilbur Findlay's mountain oysters the other day. She sautéed 'em in butter, with cream and green peppercorns. We were set to bring them over and tell you about our little surprise, but they didn't turn out so good. We decided to wait."

"Good decision." Harry wrinkled his nose. "And, what's become of all the girlie magazines?"

"Debbie's not fond of 'em. *Playboys* are in the basement. All catalogued, in boxes. High and dry."

"I'm going to town. Need anything?" Harry had forgotten his annoyance at being ignored.

"Nope. I'm going out in a minute myself, to your house in fact. Borrowed the shop vac from the garage last week. Didn't work too good. Needs a new bag. I'm takin' it back."

Harry looked down at the checkbook on the table, Nibber caught him. "I'm doin' just fine, thank you," Nibber said. "More than enough money to carry me through the winter, and if it ever stops raining, odd jobs enough to last 'til it freezes."

"Money enough for a ring?"

"A ring?" Nibber was puzzled, then caught on. "Oh, yeah. The suitcase maybe?"

"Not on your life." Harry wasn't sure Nibber was joking. "I'll go get the mail and meet you at the house. Maybe you can help me settle the nursery."

* * * *

Harry hurried off with Winston, satisfied with the side trip to Nibber's and anxious to get home. "I'll be quick," Harry promised as he drove straight through town and up to the dam where, only recently, Nibber had posted a sign reserving two spaces: **For Dam Officials Only.** Harry fretted when he first saw it, thinking some kind of state approval might be necessary, but now he'd come to like the arrangement, especially on days like this when downtown was cluttered with flatlanders.

In order to give some legitimacy to the new special parking sign, Harry leaned out the window and checked the dam gauges. Yesterday, Nibber had used his remote control to open the gate as wide as they dared, and Grand Pond was already at full height, with not an inch to spare. The spillway was madly rushing into Finger Lake, and water lapped at the base of the rotten wall near the shore.

"Can't take any more rain," Harry said to Winston. "If a bad storm comes now, we're gonna be in a fix." The dog shrugged and curled up on the seat.

Harry walked back down the road and arrived at the post office just as Jeff Molony and Mal Grandbush came out the front door. Harry tried taking cover behind a boat-trailing New Jersey suburban, but Molony and Grandbush spotted him. Harry made believe he was checking the boat's engine, and then made a quick, straight romp for the post office door. Molony stepped in the way.

"Well, now," Molony said with what Harry viewed as a bit of a sneer, "I see your good friend the dam custodian is cohabitating up on the ridge."

Harry knew perfectly well what cohabitating meant, but Mal translated anyway. "Shacking up," she said, grinning at the thought.

"It's not really any of our business." Harry struggled to be civil.

"Not at all," Mal admitted, "but I'll tell you something that *is* my business, and it's that Nibber's sudden change of lifestyle causes me to think that he just might be the Santa Claus."

"Nonsense!" Harry shook his head vigorously.

"No matter," Mal shrugged. "In any event, I have an obligation to report any and all of my suitcase suspicions to the authorities."

"You what?" Harry couldn't believe what he was hearing.

"Didn't you know?" Mal went on. "There's a federal agent in town. Been here right along, though nobody knew it. He's been looking for the suitcase. Introduced himself to me last week. Said he needed my help, and of course I'm happy to help out where I can," she said. "Unofficially, of course."

Harry didn't want to hear more, and he quickly stepped around the pair and headed for his mailbox. He pretended to fuss with the junk mail until the nosey pair had drifted off toward Knight's Store, and then he walked slowly back to the dam, deep in thought. Bad enough the murdering Nurse was still poking around looking for the money, but now the federal agent was out in the open, asking questions. In his funk, Harry forgot Winston's doughnut, and they both pouted as they slowly navigated back along the crowded Main Street.

When they reached Knight's, Harry came to a dead stop to let a woman with three leashed poodles cross the street, and he checked the rearview before moving on. "Cripes!" he yipped, slapping his forehead. The white pickup was six feet from his rear bumper. Winston sat up quickly, craned his neck out the window for a good look back, and began wagging his tail. "For the love of Pete," Harry said disgustedly, pulling the dog back inside. "It's the Nurse." He took hold of Winston's chin and made him look straight ahead. "There's just no accounting for the kinds of friends you make."

Harry at first hoped the truck would turn off at Lake Lodge, but when it stayed close behind he trounced on the accelerator, lurching Winston against the seat as they made the turn onto Shore Drive on two wheels. When the dust settled, Harry glanced in the mirror again, praying he might see the pickup continue along the main road. Instead, the Nurse had made the corner, too. A second burst spread the distance a bit, but Harry gained barely two hundred yards before he reached the house.

Nibber's Chevy was parked sideways in the driveway, and Harry wheeled around it. The garage door was wide open, and he spotted Nibber, perched at the top of the stepladder, no doubt drawing his final Joyful Waters paycheck.

"Holy shit! Get down," Harry barked as he ran into the garage. "The Nurse is right behind!" Nibber stood up straight, whacked his head on a joist, and began scrambling down the ladder. He missed the final step and sprawled on his backside on the cement floor. A half-dozen green bills fluttered in his wake, and he flailed to catch them just as the white pickup pulled in the yard.

The unsmiling Nurse walked calmly up the driveway, and Winston pranced out to greet him. Harry tried to say something, but no sound came. Instead, he turned his head back and forth from Nibber to the Nurse, trying to figure out if they'd been caught.

"Mornin'," the Nurse muttered as he stepped into the garage. "Always drive that fast?" Harry's eyes fixed on the ugly red scar on the man's face. He could only shrug.

"Let me introduce myself," the Nurse said, reaching a hand toward his pocket. Harry recoiled and was surprised to find his life story was indeed unfolding in his head. For a brief moment he regretted having wasted so much time worrying when he really should have saved it all up for a moment like this. Nibber, alternately rubbing his forehead and his backside, saw the Nurse reach for his pocket and turned to run for the back entry door.

"Not so fast." The Nurse put up his other hand. "I need to ask you boys a few questions." He pulled out his wallet, flipped it open and stuck it in front of Harry's ashen face. The identification card had the man's picture, scar and all. "*Parker Meehan*," it said, "*Special Agent, Federal Bureau of Investigation.*"

Harry examined the photograph and then the face of the man in front of him. The Nurse wasn't the Nurse at all. Nibber leaned over to have a look. His mouth fell. "Well, I'll be damned," he gushed in a little boy voice, "an honest-to-God G-man."

"We've met," Meehan said. "On the ridge, the morning after Doc O'Neil was killed. I was working undercover at the time, didn't introduce myself. If I had, I'd have said I was Lee Hemphill, the name I was using at the time." The tumbling revelations started to make Harry feel better, but then he realized they were in near as much trouble with Meehan as they would be with the Nurse, especially if the agent had seen the shower of money that followed Nibber to the floor.

Harry decided to find out. "We're having a baby," he said, feeling foolish. "I mean to say my wife and I are having a baby, and my friend here, Mr. Nabroski, was helping me get a crib down from overhead." He started to point into the rafters when his eye caught the corner of the suitcase hanging over the edge, and he went into a quick, fake coughing spate while he waved wildly with both arms, hoping Meehan wouldn't look up. "How can we help?" Harry rasped, finishing his gyrations by making an exaggerated gesture toward the cement floor.

Meehan glanced down, puzzled, then looked back at Harry and Nibber. "I'm going to be straight with you," he said. "This visit is about a suitcase full of money that belongs to the federal government." Nibber started to look up into the rafters himself, and Harry jabbed him. Meehan continued. "You probably know Doc was the head of a Boston syndicate, the Black Wharf Gang, and that he stole a great deal of money from the gang before he went to jail without telling a soul where he'd put it." They nodded in unison.

"I've been investigating Black Wharf for seven or eight years, and have the wounds to prove it." Meehan put a finger on the side of his face. "We've about shut them down, but the missing money is a very big loose end. We've waited three years, thinking Doc might lead us to it when he got out of Ray Brook in March." He shook his head. "I tailed him from prison, and I hate to admit it, but he gave me the slip. Must have arranged for a half-dozen rental cars, and kept swapping. When I was certain I'd lost him, I headed straight for Maine and the O'Neil place, thinking he'd bring the money home and I could catch him here."

"What happened?" Nibber was still proudly holding Meehan's wallet.

"I checked in at Lake Lodge and drove over here, parked on Shore Drive, and walked to the O'Neil house. I was about an hour too late. Somebody had shot him, so I just hung around in the woods and watched, figuring the state boys would find the money and I could claim it from them."

Harry interrupted. "You said 'somebody' shot Doc. Wasn't that somebody his wife?"

"Another whole story," Meehan said. "You might not know this, but I'm not the only outsider who's been poking around for the money. There's another guy, Michael Corrado, and I'm tellin' you, he's one big, bad boy. He'd kill for any amount of money in a heartbeat. They call him the Nurse. He and Doc got crossways when Doc took the gang's money."

Harry looked at Nibber, remembering the day of Salome's trial when Nibber suggested the Nurse might be the real killer. "So, I take it you think the Nurse shot Doc O'Neil," Harry said, trying not to stutter.

"I do," Meehan said matter-of-factly. "He wanted that money, and he wanted to get even with Doc. Add that to the fact that he was in Belfry that same night. Checked in at Lake Lodge a good four hours before I got there. Motive and opportunity, plain as day. As for the means, I suppose it's possible the gun came from Doc, but more likely it belonged to the Nurse, just the kind of guy who'd carry a piece with the numbers filed off."

"All well and good," Harry said skeptically, "but it doesn't explain why Salome confessed."

"Simple." Meehan was quick with an answer. "She was terrified. The Nurse probably threatened to kill her if she didn't go along. Or, who knows, maybe he offered her a reward for taking the fall."

Harry pressed on, trying to fill in the blanks. "So, why didn't you tell this whole story to the police?"

"Two reasons. First, I had no real proof. Second, the murder wasn't any of my business. My job was to recover the money. The state boys took care of the murder."

"So where's the Nurse now?"

"Back in Revere Beach. We've got a tail on him. Came to Belfry three times in all. Used a different rental each time. Spent his time poking in the woods near the O'Neil property. Hasn't been back since his last inspection, after the snow melted."

Harry shot a glance at Nibber, and Meehan leaned against Harry's workbench. "Enough of that," Meehan said, folding his arms. "Let's get down to business." He stared intently, first at Harry, then at Nibber. "As I said, I've been undercover since March, and gotten nowhere. The only thing I know is what everybody else knows. Somebody around here has got the suitcase and that somebody is giving the money away. Last week I stopped playing Lee Hemphill and came out of the closet, so to speak. Started asking questions."

"So, what have you learned?" Nibber was pretending to be a G-man, Harry could tell.

"Well, if you don't mind me saying, this whole town is nuts. Everybody thinks they know everything, but it turns out nobody knows anything."

"Same problem trying to operate a dam," Nibber jumped in.

Meehan didn't get it, and went on. "I started with Trooper Brown and the sheriff's deputy, Hallowell. Neither one has a clue about the money, but they gave me a list of Belfry people who might be able to help. I've already talked with a few of them, including the librarian, Grandbush." He stopped, shook his head. "Now, there's a real piece of work," he said. "She's got no end of theories on who has the suitcase. I know, because I've tracked down most of 'em and they're all dead ends." He grinned and pointed at Nibber. "Yesterday, she fingered you. Says you've been acting real strange."

"Anybody around here could tell you *that* was a dead end," Harry offered.

Nibber ignored Harry and pointed into the driveway at his tilting Chevy. "You don't think I'd be driving that heap if I had a pile of money, do you?" He paused, and then a second light came on. "If you're investigating strange people, you should really talk with the real estate developer, Jeff Molony. He's really quite odd, and a sleazebag, besides." Nibber grinned.

Meehan made a note, and his face grew serious. "Deputy Hallowell told me you boys were on the ridge the night Doc was killed," he said, peering closely. Harry looked away. Sure enough, Kelly had finally found someone with a need to know. "That reminded me," Meehan continued, "I met the two of you the next day, up on the ridge, with your dog."

"That would be Winston," Nibber filled in. Meehan reached down to pat Winston's head, and the dog rolled onto his back, all feet in the air.

"So, you know everything I know," Meehan moved even closer. "Now it's your turn." He put a finger on

Nibber's chest, then Harry's. "Is there anything at all you boys would like to tell me about the suitcase?"

"Not a thing." Harry answered quickly, pleased that he wasn't lying. "But, tell me," he asked, "when you do find the money, what will happen to the person who has it?"

"All depends," Meehan said. "You see, there's a big problem with this whole case. First of all, we don't actually know how much money is in the suitcase. Could be a half-million or more, we just don't know. So far, whoever has the money hasn't spent very much, maybe a few thousand on various charities. If they gave it up voluntarily, I suppose we'd just say 'thank you' and let 'em go."

Harry was pleased. Meehan obviously didn't have a clue about Nibber's salary for the repair of Joyful Waters, or the subsidy for Debbie's farm.

"On the other hand," Meehan went on. "If we have to work any harder to get the suitcase back, I can promise you they'll go down for theft of federal property." Harry stifled a gulp, and Meehan turned to leave, then stepped back to retrieve his wallet from Nibber. "Here," he said, pulling out a card and handing it to Nibber. "If you boys hear anything about the money, anything at all, give me a call. Right away."

"Yes, sir." Nibber saluted, and Harry thought he looked a bit silly. Winston followed Meehan to his car, considered his options, and elected to join Harry and Nibber as they ran down the steps and into the house.

"Oh boy," Harry exclaimed when he burst through the door. "Do I ever have news for you!"

Diane was mopping fur balls from under Harry's chair. "Too late," she grinned. "Nibber told me an hour ago, when he returned the shop vac."

"It's not about Debbie moving in with Nibber," Harry said. "It's about the Nurse." Diane stopped mopping, and Harry gushed it out. "The Nurse is not the Nurse. He's the FBI guy. His name's Parker Meehan, who called himself Lee Hemphill, and he believes the *real* Nurse, that would be Michael Corrado, is the one who shot Doc."

"For god's sake, slow down," Diane said, pushing the two men ahead of her onto the porch where he repeated the entire conversation, including Meehan's report that Mal Grandbush had accused Nibber and, in turn, Nibber had fingered Bolony.

"That wasn't very nice," Diane said.

"Won't matter," Nibber giggled. "If Meehan runs that one down, he'll get nowhere. Any number of people will testify that Bolony never gave away a cent, to anybody."

Diane walked to the porch rail. "As far as Meehan thinking the Nurse killed Doc goes," she said as they watched an osprey circle overhead, "we should let it go. It's over and done with. Salome did it, that's that, and she's moving on. So should we." The osprey folded its wings and dove out of sight into the water, emerging a moment later with a foot-long fish.

"Makes me think of Meehan," Harry said. "One of these days he's gonna swoop down and snatch the suitcase."

"It's a good thing we decided to cool it for awhile," Diane said. "How much money have we got left, anyway?"

Nibber had made most of the withdrawals, and he answered. "About half, I'd say. One of these days, we really should count it."

Harry stared at Diane. Her belly was beginning to grow, and he felt a sudden protective impulse. "Count it or not," he said, "we've got to *move* it." He looked at Nibber, expecting him to say he'd been thinking and wasn't disappointed.

"I've been thinkin'," Nibber blurted, "that we ought to move the suitcase to the dam, put it in that steel toolbox I made."

"Don't be silly. Much too public," Harry said, flatly.

"That's the whole point," Nibber came back. "Nobody will think to look for the suitcase right under their noses, and besides, if anybody goes out on the dam, they're bound to be seen. At the same time, if one of us goes out there, nobody will think a thing about it. Public is perfect. On top of that, the catwalk is chained and locked and the toolbox has a padlock as well. I measured it yesterday. The suitcase will fit just fine, with plenty of extra room for the tools."

Harry looked at Diane and waited until she nodded her head.

"Okay, fine," he said, looking at Nibber. "You do it. Do it tonight."

22

Harry was up pacing around the house most of the night, fretting about the coming storm. He had barely drifted off to sleep when the telephone rang. He sat up straight in bed and opened one eye to look at the clock. Five thirty. "Who in hell would be calling at this ungodly hour?" he sputtered.

"Nibber," Diane muttered from under her pillow.

"Happy Labor Day," the cheery voice said.

"What's happy about it?"

"Well, I've got bad news and good news," Nibber replied. "Which one you want first?"

"Bad."

"Okay. State dam people called a few minutes ago. Hurricane Carla is off Portland, headed straight this way. She might be a tropical storm by the time she gets here, but we're still in for tons of rain. They want us to hold back as much water as we can. Already some flooding down below."

Harry sat on the edge of the bed and reached back to poke Diane, then Winston. "Told you guys," he said proudly, "Clara's coming." He'd been watching the storm for a week. The first two of the season's hurricanes fizzled out in the Carolinas, but Clara had bounced along the Atlantic coast for a couple of days before a low-pressure system invited her in. He made the dire prediction last night when he gave the barometer a final tap before going to bed. The needle was headed for the tank.

Diane mumbled a word of praise for Harry's prediction, and Winston crept into the warm spot Harry left behind and played dead. Harry went back to Nibber. "I don't give a damn what the state boys say," he said. "We've got no room to move and I don't want to change things an inch."

"Least we can do is have a look," Nibber said. "Debbie's working breakfast at the Sunrise. I'm taking her in a few minutes. Meet you after." Harry was about to hang up when Nibber's voice returned. "Oh, yes," he said, "more bad news." Harry grunted. "Remember that big pine blowdown in Mosher Stream last spring," Nibber asked, "the one we pegged onto the bank when we couldn't get it out?"

"She's loose, I'll bet."

"Yup. Allie Knight called from the store last night. Said the high water had set her adrift. It's monstrous. It was snagged up when Allie called, but she won't hold. Headed for the spillway."

"Can't do a thing about it now," Harry said, jabbing at Winston, still playing dead. "And by the way, what's the good news?"

"Most of the flatlanders left town ahead of the storm."

Harry grinned, hung up, and pulled on his clothes before he yanked Winston's front paws to get him off the bed. "We'll see what we see," he said to Diane, bending to peck her on the cheek. "I'll come back for you. We'll have a late breakfast at the Sunrise."

* * * *

Winston sat nervously on the passenger seat as Harry crept along Shore Drive, skirting fallen limbs and several places where swollen streams had jumped their culverts. The wipers couldn't handle the rain, and green leaves, ripped by the wind, stuck to the windshield. The main road was no better. Ditches on both sides were overflowing, and angry black sheets of water raced over the pavement.

At Lake Lodge, Harry took his eyes off the road long enough to glance into the parking lot. The white pickup loomed like a ghost, reminding him that Parker Meehan had been working out in the open for weeks, showing his badge, asking questions, searching for the money.

The worrisome thought was driven away by a growing wind that filled the air with swirling debris. Up ahead, in the lights of Knight's Store, Harry saw figures gathered around the lone gas pump, filling cars, trucks, and assorted cans. When he passed by the store, he cracked the window to listen for a generator, but there was no sound. Good, he thought. Power's still on. Dam gate will work if we decide to move it.

Up ahead, Aidan Brown's cruiser was parked near the bridge, blue lights circling. Draped in a yellow slicker, the trooper directed one car at a time over the narrow span, and when he recognized Harry's red

Toyota, waved him in to the reserved space next to Nibber's forlorn Chevy.

The wild weather had Winston in a state, and he slinked out of the truck inches behind Harry, sticking close. At the entrance to the catwalk, they stopped to watch as a thick, fast-moving sheet of water leaped out over the dam, crashing in a thunderous roar into Finger Lake. The spillway was well over the shore-side bank, and a whole new river was breaking a new course behind the crumbling wall.

Harry raised a hand up to keep the water out of his eyes and saw Nibber at the end of the walkway, hunched over the controls. Harry grabbed the rails and started out. Winston tested the rattling aluminum deck with one paw, shook his head, and turned back to sit in the grass. When Harry was halfway out, Nibber heard him and turned. "She's shorted," he yelled above the wind, holding the remote clicker in the air. "Rain in the main box."

Harry inched up close. "Never liked the damn thing," he hissed in Nibber's ear. "Hard-wire it, back the way it was."

"Fine, but I'll need a screwdriver and a pair of pliers."

Harry started back along the catwalk, and Nibber called after him. "Wait!" he said. "The tool box is gone." Harry wheeled around, hadn't noticed on the way out. "Blowdown took it," Nibber shrugged. "Aidan said it hit the box like a battering ram. About an hour ago."

"Cripes." Harry was back face-to-face with Nibber. "The suitcase?"

"Gone, too, I guess." Nibber seemed nonchalant, put a wet arm around Harry's shoulder. "The box was open in the back. Suitcase must have fallen out. Don't worry," he added quickly. "I'm pretty sure we'll find the money."

"Don't worry? My God man, if the suitcase fell out in this madness, it was bound to open up. Don't forget, it was already damaged where we tried to pry it open."

"Where *you* tried to pry it open," Nibber corrected.

"Never mind," Harry sputtered. "If we can find the money, so can the rest of Belfry. Tens and twenties will be washing up on shore for weeks."

"Stop fussing and get me the tools." Nibber wiped the rain out of his hair. "We've gotta get this gate up a notch or two. Frig the state boys."

Harry used both hands to pull himself against the wind along the catwalk. Winston was waiting at the other end, soaking wet and impatient. Harry put him in the cab, wiped him with a towel, and rummaged in the back for what he needed.

"No sense for me to wait out here," he said when he handed Nibber the tools. "Saw Kelly Hallowell up on the bridge. I need to talk to her. Signal if you need me." Nibber made a tent out of his raincoat and bent back over the controls.

At the end of the catwalk, Harry stopped to look at the dam wall. The giant blowdown had turned lengthwise when it fell, and its thick trunk was stretched across the full span of the spillway, deflecting even more water into the new river behind the wall. Over the screaming wind, he heard the clatter of large rocks, freed by the rushing water, carving the bottom deeper by the second.

When Harry clambered onto the road, he could see a crowd had begun to gather near Knight's Store, getting storm supplies, he figured, and trying to get a close look at the howling water. Aidan had moved down toward the store and was doing his best to keep people from walking up to the bridge where Kelly Hallowell had taken a perimeter post.

"You know I could never let you be here unless you were on the Dam Committee," Kelly said when Harry joined her at the rail.

"But I *am* on the Dam Committee." Harry tried to be nice. "Although at the moment I wish I wasn't."

"What's Nibber up to?" Kelly brushed at the rain running off her nose and pointed to the dam.

"Trying to raise the gate a bit," Harry explained, squinting at the white water as it boiled all the way up the shore beyond what remained of Molony's docks. "Where's Bolony?" he asked, innocently.

"Mr. Molony was here with the Deacon a half-hour ago," she said. "They left when Molony's pontoon boat broke its mooring. He took another boat from his armada to chase it. I told him not to go. It's not safe. I don't worry much about the Deacon. He hasn't been near the water since he was twice saved in that scuba incident." She looked up and down the road. "He has to be around here somewhere."

"Bolony can't be a happy camper at the moment." Harry ventured.

"Nope." Kelly allowed herself a tiny grin. "Had some real colorful things to say about your Dam Committee."

"The Dam Committee's got nothing to do with Clara," Harry countered. "Maybe now he'll wish he'd gotten behind the spillway repair project."

"I suppose there's lots of people who'll have second thoughts when this is over," Kelly said, staring out over the frothing water.

"I see Parker Meehan is still around," Harry said, gently prying.

"Saw him at the Sunrise last night." Kelly answered without a pause. "Said he was giving up his investigation, pulling stakes. Even with Mal's help, he's plum run out of leads. Was going back to Boston last night, but then the storm came, and he decided to hole up at the Lodge one more night."

"They'll never find that money." Harry meant what he said. "Or for that matter, who killed Doc."

Kelly perked up. "Reminds me," she said, "my friend at the phone company called yesterday. She checked the records." Harry pulled back the hood of his slicker. "The only call that went in or out of the O'Neil house that night was the 911 that Salome made." She shrugged. "Guess that's a dead end, too."

The wind was blowing water sideways off Finger Lake, straight in their faces, and Harry turned and shut his eyes. "Thanks for chasing it down," he said finally, pulling the hood back over his head. "I'd best go see how Nibber's making out." She nodded, and he had barely turned to leave when a wailing shriek came from down the shore, along the edge of the spillway. Kelly heard it, too.

"Someone's in trouble," she shouted. Harry squinted in the direction of the yelling and thought he saw the figure of a man, near the water's edge, in a small clump of trees.

"Wait here," he said. "I'll get a rope from the truck, and we'll go down and see." She nodded, and when he and Winston returned, all three headed down the steep bank on the shore side of the spillway. Kelly was in front, flailing her arms to keep her balance. They had barely reached level ground when she turned back.

"It's the Deacon," she exclaimed, eyes wide. "And he's holding a suitcase!" She moved back toward Harry, cocked her head and started to speak. "You don't suppose ..."

Harry cut her off. "You can be sure. It's *the* suitcase."

Kelly seemed confused, then gathered herself. "Let's go."

"Wait!" Harry grabbed her by the holster belt. "Listen to me," he said firmly, bending to peer directly in her face. "Get yourself as close as you can, but don't let him see you. I have an idea. You've gotta trust me. If this works, you could become Maine's Deputy Sheriff of the Year."

"What?" Kelly was puzzled.

"Trust me," he said again, worrying that she might get stubborn, but instead she shrugged and angled off through a thick stand of alders. He waited to make sure she didn't change her mind, then moved along the shore with Winston until he saw the Deacon, knee-deep in the foaming water, standing on a tiny spit of land in the middle of the flow, holding the suitcase in one hand and clutching a spindly tree with the other.

The pieces were coming together in Harry's head. When the suitcase dropped out of the toolbox it must have gone through the spillway and fetched up on a clump of trees a short way from shore. The Deacon must have seen it, and in the time it took him to wade out and get it, the fast water widened the gap. Now, he didn't dare to venture back.

The Deacon hadn't seen them, and was still sending mournful howls in the direction of the bridge. Harry looked to be sure Kelly had found a place to hide, and Winston nodded toward a mid-sized pine near the water. Harry spotted her broad hips, sticking out like twin burls at the bottom of the tree. "Find a bigger one." He spoke up as loudly as he dared, pointing to an aged pine even closer to the shore.

Harry waited for her to move, then stepped into the open and followed Winston, already at the water's edge, racing back and forth along the bank, barking. The Deacon saw him, then Harry, and made a screaming plea. "Save me!"

Harry pulled the looped rope off his shoulder and gauged the distance. The gulf was at least ten feet wide and growing each time a new chunk of soil broke off and dissolved in the furious current. "Drop the suitcase," he yelled across the water. "You'll need both hands."

The Deacon drew the heavy case up to his chest and changed hands, desperately groping to get a new hold on the tiny tree. "No way," he shouted back. "It's mine." At that moment, a rock under his foot suddenly washed away, and as he scrambled to regain his footing. Harry could see the terror in his eyes. The Deacon begged again. "Please, the rope," he bellowed.

Harry's mind raced. He wasn't about to let the man drown, but he'd never get a better chance to make things right. He moved to the very edge of the water. "I'll give you the rope," he shouted loud enough for Kelly to hear, "but first, you tell me why you killed Doc O'Neil."

The roaring of the wind and rain suddenly seemed to let up, and Harry waited, didn't move. An astonished look came over the Deacon's face, and his eyes grew wide. "You're crazy," he finally hollered back, clinging to the suitcase with one hand and the tree with the other.

Harry waited a second or two, then shouted even louder. "Listen, you two-timing, church-thieving son-of-a-bitch, either you answer my question or I'll leave you right here."

The Deacon sobbed. "Come on, Harry," he begged as the rain picked up. "For the love of God, you know I can't swim."

"God saved you from drowning once," Harry shot back. "But he's not likely to make the same mistake twice." He turned around, took a step back toward the bridge.

"Wait!" the Deacon screamed. Harry paused, turned his head. The Deacon glanced furtively up and down the shore. Then the words tumbled out.

"Okay, I shot Doc." He coughed up some water and went on. "So what? The man was worthless trash. Had it coming. Nobody else got hurt. Salome got off. I couldn't have." He stopped, heaved a sigh, seemed to consider what he'd just said. "Anyway, nobody can prove it."

"I think I can," Harry mumbled to himself as he uncoiled the rope and tossed an end over the abyss. In one wild motion, the Deacon let go of the tree, grabbed the rope, and twisted it around his arm. Harry gave a mighty heave, and the Deacon came over the raging current, face first, dragging the suitcase and spewing water.

Kelly had left her hiding place, and was waiting on the bank with handcuffs. As the Deacon climbed awkwardly onto his feet, she raised her head to look in his face and began reciting the Miranda. He mumbled that he understood, then promptly ignored his right to keep his mouth shut. "You heard?" he asked in disbelief.

Kelly smiled sweetly and held out the cuffs. "Every word," she said as she fastened his hands behind his back, tested the arrangement with a good shake, and eased him down on the soaking grass. When he was settled, she motioned Harry to move away. "I radioed Brown," she said when they were out of earshot. "He's coming down to help." She bent to scratch Winston on his wet head, then looked back at Harry. "Thanks," she said simply.

"This has been one helluva day," Aidan said as he greeted them, brushing globs of mud off his trousers. "Caught a hurricane, a murderer and the suitcase bandit, all in one day." He grinned and looked at Kelly. "I'm not entirely clear on the murder. You?"

"Bits and pieces, but I suspect Harry will fill us in," she answered. "In the meantime, there's plenty enough to book him." She nodded toward the suitcase and the Deacon, huddled on the lawn, shivering. "You take him," she said. "I'll take the money."

The rain and wind had slowed, and the glimmer of a red sun was rising over Grand Pond. Aidan went to yank the gangly Deacon onto his feet and pointed him up the hill. Kelly grabbed the dripping suitcase, tested the weight, and then brought it up to her chest in a grunting bear hug. Even with half the money gone, it seemed to Harry that the soaking had made the case even heavier than it was the night he and Nibber had lugged it over the ridge. He started to offer to help, thought better of it, then followed the odd parade up the bank, stopping once to look back along the spillway. The old shore wall was entirely gone, and flashes of white water curled around the remaining hunks of rotted cement. With the abutment gone, the flood had made its own free course, devouring much of Molony's property and eating at the Finger Lake shoreline for hundreds of yards before the raging water played out.

Up ahead, Aidan followed the handcuffed Deacon, and Kelly slogged a few steps behind, grimly hugging the suitcase. When they reached the top, Harry heard the familiar whine of the dam gate. Nibber had gotten the thing running. It was too late to save the spillway, but lowering the water would at least lighten the heavy load on Grand Pond.

Harry spotted Parker Meehan on the bridge, pinned to the rail by an animated Mal Grandbush. Meehan made a plea with his eyes to be rescued, and Harry arrived in time to hear Mal explain to the hapless agent that the Deacon had been on her list of suitcase suspects all along. "Just hadn't gotten to him yet," she said as Meehan gently lifted her arm off the rail and escaped underneath. Mal continued jabbering into the vacant space, then worked her way down the bridge, yakking away to anyone she met.

Aidan had moved his cruiser, and it was parked just off the bridge where the road widened, closer to Knight's Store. Harry kept his head down and followed the procession through the gauntlet of curious sightseers. When they got to the cruiser, Aidan reached out to open a rear door, and then jumped back. Harry peered inside. Henry McLaughlin was stretched out over the back seat. "Must have gone on a toot when the storm started," Aidan grinned apologetically, "then found a safe place to sleep it off." He tugged at a boot hanging off the seat, and poor Henry sat slowly upright. "Move over," Aidan said as Kelly reached up and put her hand on the Deacon's head before folding him onto the seat.

Henry seemed pleased to have company. "Mornin' Governor," he said cheerfully. "Sun's out. She'll be a fine day." The Deacon curled his lip and turned to stare out the foggy window.

Aidan took charge. "Okay," he said, looking at Meehan. "I'll take the prisoner. You take the suitcase."

"No!" Meehan was firm. "You take the suitcase, too. We'll count the money at the station and I'll give you a receipt." He turned to Harry. "A word, my good man, if you don't mind."

Harry followed them to the back of the car, and they spoke for several minutes before Aidan motioned Meehan toward the front seat. "We'd better get going," he said, "before this crowd gets any bigger." Most had left the bridge and were circling the cruiser, trying to get a glimpse of the notorious suitcase thief.

Harry sidled up to Kelly, doing her best to shoo everybody away. He bent to whisper. "They don't know he's a murderer as well," he said. She was set to reply when a shout came from the bridge. It was Nibber.

"Wait for me!" Nibber yelled, shedding his raincoat and leaving a trail of water as he ran up the road. He arrived just as the cruiser and the sheriff's car pulled away. "Mal just told me the Deacon caught the suitcase," he said. "Tell me all about it."

Harry suddenly realized Nibber had been fussing with the switches all the while and had missed the entire show. "Let's get out of these wet clothes. I'll fill you in at the Sunrise."

"Yeah," Nibber said with a grin. "And I can fill you in on a few things of my own."

23

Diane knelt on the kitchen floor, drying Winston with a towel, warm from the oven. "Tell me something," she asked, looking up, "how on earth did you know the Deacon killed Doc?" Winston was on his back, his lips hanging open as he lolled his head toward Harry, waiting for an answer.

"Deduction," Harry said, shedding his wet clothes in a heap and heading upstairs. "I'll spell it all out at the Sunrise."

"There's plenty to spell out," Diane called after him. "The day's not half over and the world's gone completely mad. First, the hurricane, then Mal Grandbush calls to say the Deacon got caught with the suitcase. And as if that wasn't enough, you come home and tell me the Deacon has admitted killing Doc O'Neil. That's a lot to swallow all at once."

Harry took a quick shower, came back downstairs. They stood for a minute by the window, gazing out over the lake. Clara had left as quickly as she had come, and the sudden, warm sun raised a lacey mist over the water. "The mysteries will lift with the fog," Harry smiled. "Let's get going."

They rode with the windows open and listened to the birds chirping and the sounds of sump pumps gushing water out basement windows. Road crews were out filling the washouts, and outside their houses, people were raking green leaves and pulling broken branches off their roofs.

Debbie was waiting outside the Sunrise, and she ran to put her arms around Harry's neck. "Now, don't you worry yourself," she consoled. "I promise you, everything will turn out just fine."

"You know?" Harry was surprised.

"Mal called."

"My God, the woman must have the entire village on speed dial."

"Told me how you and Kelly caught the Deacon red-handed with the suitcase. Said she was sad the donations will dry up, but I can tell, she thinks the Deacon was Santa Claus and she's real proud of her role in solving the mystery."

"She didn't have a role," Harry grumbled. "Besides, for once she doesn't know the half of it. Where's Nibber?"

"Called a few minutes ago. He's on his way."

Except for a half dozen of the all-day crowd, sipping longnecks at the bar, the Sunrise was empty. "Kitchen's closed 'til four," Debbie said. "Emily's gone home, but I'll hustle something up. Salad for Diane and me. Leftover meatloaf for you guys, and I'll put some rings in the fryer." She nodded toward their corner booth.

"We'll take a table, if you don't mind." Diane grinned, patting her belly. "I don't think I can still fit in the booth." Harry grinned and bent to kiss her cheek just as Nibber came through the door, out of breath.

"You poor, dear boy," Debbie cooed, combing his wet hair with her fingers. "Out there working in the most miserable weather while everybody else was having a high old time for themselves."

"I haven't exactly been on a picnic," Harry sighed as they moved to the table under the wagon wheel. "We need a special meeting of the Dam Committee, plus one. And we need it now."

"Be right back," Debbie said, heading off to the kitchen.

One by one, the good old boys began to weave out the door, and by the time Debbie returned, the place was empty. "Thanks to Grandbush, you already know about the suitcase," Harry said, looking at Nibber, then Diane, "but what you don't know is that along the way, the Deacon confessed to killing Doc."

"Sweet Jesus!" Nibber's mouth fell open, and an exclamation point catsup nib splashed onto the front of his Dam Committee T-shirt. He looked down quickly, seemed pleased with the accent, and left it alone. "Boy, I sure missed a whole lot when my head was stuck in the dam controls."

Harry began to relate the details of the confession, but Diane interrupted. "You should start at the very beginning," she said, "and tell us how you suspected the Deacon in the first place."

"Well, you know I never thought Salome was the killer," Harry explained. "A liar, maybe, but not a killer, and after the trial, I was pretty sure someone else had shot Doc."

"So, how's that?" Nibber asked.

"Think about it," Harry said. "Her testimony about Doc wanting her to fetch the suitcase didn't make any sense. A man who goes to jail to protect a pile of money doesn't turn around the next day and try to give it to his wife. If you ask me, it was the other way around. Salome wanted the money, and when he refused to give it to her, she stopped visiting."

"Speculation," Diane interjected lawyer-like. "Never could prove it."

"Besides," Nibber chipped in. "That theory of yours makes Salome *more* of a suspect, not less, and it doesn't begin to explain how you got around to thinking it was the Deacon who shot him."

"I'm getting to all that," Harry said impatiently. "You see, I never thought the Deacon was Salome's spiritual advisor. He was at her house altogether too much for praying. They were having an affair, plain as day."

"Speculation!" Diane objected again.

Debbie tried to help out. "Well," she said, "at the end of the day, at least there's the confession."

"Confession's no good," Diane said. "No judge will have it."

Nibber agreed. "It's true. The man was being tortured at the time."

"You're right," Harry made a small smile, "except if the Deacon is as stupid as I think he is, he's confessing again right now at the Watford Police Station, where I presume his life is not being threatened at all."

Diane still wasn't sure. "Even so," she said, "it'll take more than a confession to charge him with a murder, especially after somebody else has been tried and acquitted."

"What else you got?" Nibber looked at Harry. "Like, maybe something solid."

"I'll give you the three things I gave Brown, Hallowell and Meehan this morning after they put the Deacon in the cruiser." Harry held up one finger. "First, the Deacon was there when Doc got shot, and here's how I know. Salome said she called him after she shot Doc, but Kelly told me this morning at the dam that the only call in or out of the house that night was Salome's 911, and we know it was made at ten after five. When Kelly got there ten minutes later, the Deacon was already there. Even if Salome had called him, there's no way he could have gotten from his house on the East Road to the O'Neils' in ten minutes. And on top of that," he looked at Nibber, "we saw the Deacon's army Jeep parked in front of Kelly's cruiser that night on the ridge. If he'd come after the shooting, he'd been parked behind her."

"So," Nibber interrupted, "he was there, but don't forget, Salome wasn't expecting Doc home from Ray Brook until the next day. The murder couldn't have been planned."

"You're wrong," Harry answered. "As I see it, the two of them planned to get rid of Doc and make off with the money the next day, but Doc came home a day early, saw the Deacon's Jeep, hid the suitcase, and stormed into the house, ready to kill."

"What was the Deacon doing there a day early?" Debbie asked.

"Practicing with his gun," Nibber suggested with a grin.

"Shush!" Diane shook her head.

"Suspect so," Harry agreed, raising a second finger. "Salome admitted she was in the bedroom at the time. And here's another thing: I'm almost certain they can show the murder weapon belonged to the Deacon, not Doc, and I'll tell you why. The day I picked up the Deacon to work at Joyful Waters, I admired his gun collection, and he let me have a copy of the catalogue from last year's gun show in Watford where he had this big display. I wasn't much interested at the time, but later I went through the catalogue and found a photo of his Ruger. I remembered that at the trial, the police expert, Paradis, pointed out a scratch on the wooden grip. Sure enough, the catalogue picture has the same scratch. I'll bet a year's worth of meatloaf that when they get a warrant for the Deacon's house, they won't find the gun in his collection because it's in the evidence bag."

"Wow!" Diane finally seemed convinced.

Harry beamed. "*You're* the one who found the third clue," he said, pointing to Nibber. "After you made the wall repairs at the O'Neils', you told us the bullet hole in the two-by-four came from high up, maybe too high for Salome to be the one who handled the gun." Harry looked around the table. "How tall is the Deacon?" He answered his own question. "Pretty damn tall, and since Nibber didn't replace the two-by-four, all they have to do is pull off the sheetrock and do a little recalculating on the trajectory."

"Amazing," Diane said, "and now I'm left to wonder what becomes of poor Salome."

"Don't feel sorry for her," Harry said. "She can't be tried for murder again, but I'm guessing the sleazy Deacon will implicate her as an accomplice. The evidence sure points that way. Her trial was a complete fraud. She lied, left and right. You can be sure she'll at least go down for perjury."

Diane thought a minute, and then looked at the others. "This is probably the last fake meeting of the Dam Committee plus one," she said sadly. "Nibber doesn't need any more dating excuses, and we've lost the money." She shrugged. "At least we can be thankful you two are together." She looked at Nibber and Debbie. "And, I must admit, it is a relief not to have everybody in town breathing down our necks, looking for the suitcase." She thought some more. "Come to think of it, there's some weird justice in having the Deacon take the rap."

Harry grinned at the thought. "It is pretty funny when you think about it. Even though he'll be telling the truth when he says it wasn't him, he's already a proven liar. Nobody, not even Bolony, will believe him when he says he had nothing to do with taking the money in the first place."

Nibber snatched the last onion ring, showering it in salt. "Speaking of the suitcase," he said, winking at Debbie, "I told you I had some filling in to do."

"What say?" Harry sat straight up.

"Well, I'll tell you." Nibber was plainly enjoying the moment. "I took the suitcase to the dam that night, like we all agreed."

"*As* we all agreed." Diane interrupted.

"That's right," Nibber went on, "just like we all agreed. But when I got to the dam, the Deacon and Bolony were out for a walk, checking the spillway, I'd guess. They saw me carrying the suitcase, even waved, so I pretended it was full of tools and went out to fuss with the controls. After a few minutes, I carried it back with me to the truck."

"So, where is it now?" Harry brightened.

"When I got home that night, Debbie and I talked about it. We were afraid they might have figured things out, so we decided I should take the suitcase right back, that same night. I did. Made a big fuss over locking it in the toolbox, just to see what would happen.

Harry groaned. "We know what happened."

"Well, anyway. At least we know now that the Deacon must have seen me," Nibber said. "Otherwise, he wouldn't have been keeping an eye on the toolbox during the flood."

"That settles that," Diane said, shrugging her shoulders. "What's done is done."

"Not quite," Nibber glanced at the door before he got up and walked to their favorite booth in the corner. He turned and made a small bow toward Harry before he lifted the padded top off one of the seats and pulled two cloth grocery bags from the space below. "We didn't want to tell you guys," he said, plopping the bags on the table. "Didn't want to upset Diane in her condition," he said, "and I never like upsetting Harry, in any case."

Harry and Diane stood to peer in the bags. They were filled with money.

Nibber and Debbie began laughing at their own joke and waltzed around the table, clapping hands. Harry and Diane stared at each other, mouths wide, then joined in.

Suddenly, in the midst of the celebration, Harry's face grew serious. "Wait a damn minute," he said, turning to Nibber. "I watched when Kelly lugged that suitcase up the banking this morning. It was heavy, and dripping wet when they put it in the cruiser. It's probably being opened right now at the Watford station. If they're not going to find the money in there, what on earth are they going to find?"

Nibber giggled, slapped Harry on the back. "*Playboy* magazines," he said. "The duplicates."